*To the team at Mary King's Close –
many thanks for the special tour and the useful
insights into everyday life in the 17th century.*

Praise for Philip Caveney

THE SEBASTIAN DARKE ADVENTURES

"Unputdownable! The comedy in the book makes it very enjoyable and you will keep turning page after page."
CBBC Newsround

"It all adds up to an amusing and action-packed tale of loyalty, unexpected love and trouble around every bend."
Publisher's Weekly

"...zips along with plenty of jokes, outrageous moments of melodrama and odd spots of violence of the type that never really seems to hurt. A sequel is promised soon; readers who enjoy this book, and there should be many, can start looking forward to it now."
Nicolas Tucker, Times Educational Supplement.

THE ALEC DEVLIN ADVENTURES

"A fast-paced action adventure that literally brings the archaelogy and history of a lost civilisation to life."
Writeaway

"Philip Caveney is an author who knows what appeals to young boys and in Maze of Death he certainly delivers."
Book Zone For Boys

"This story will appeal to adventure and fantasy fans from Intermediate age upwards."
Story Time Books

ONE

Tom stood in the pouring rain with the other kids from his class and waited for the coach. It was April, but felt cold enough for December. His classmates, boys and girls alike, were bundled up in heavy coats and parkas; they'd known what to expect. Tom had only his maroon blazer, which was already wet through.

It was hard not to feel sorry for himself. He hated Edinburgh, he hated his new school and he hated his classmates. And, what was worse, they hated him.

Oh, he could see that under different circumstances, Edinburgh would be a really cool place to visit. But he was here against his will. Only a week ago, he'd been in Manchester, hanging out with his friends, going to the movies, playing computer games, all the usual stuff. Any excuse not to spend too much time at home. He'd known for a long time that something was wrong between his parents; he'd suffered their long, deep silences, the sudden arguments that blew up out of nowhere but he'd chosen to stay out of it, telling himself that they were adults; they were supposed to know what they were doing . . .

And then, one Friday, he strolled out of school, looking forward to the weekend, and his Mum was waiting for him, sitting in the passenger seat of a car he'd never seen before, a sleek black Alfa Romeo. There was this guy at the wheel of the car, a thickset man with a scrubby beard and receding hair. Mum wound down the window and said, 'Hi, Tom, get in.'

So he climbed into the back seat, bewildered, and Mum gestured at the driver and said, 'This is Hamish,' like it was supposed to mean something. Then Hamish gunned the engine and they set off.

'Where we going?' Tom asked apprehensively.

'Scotland,' she said, breezily, like she'd just announced they were nipping down the shops. 'Edinburgh. We're going to have a bit of a holiday.'

'For the weekend, you mean?'

'Umm . . . maybe a bit longer.'

'But . . . it's the middle of term,' he reminded her.

'Don't worry about that. I think you're entitled to a few days off every now and then.'

But of course, it was more than that. On the long . . . the very long journey North, Mum gradually revealed more and more about what was going on. She and Dad hadn't been getting on for a long time now. They'd drifted apart. She'd met Hamish through work, three months back. He was a rep, a kind of travelling salesman for a company that made shower fittings. He was based in Edinburgh, a really cool city. She kept saying that last bit as though trying to convince Tom that what they were doing was a good idea. Or maybe she was just trying to convince herself.

Anyway, she went on, she and Hamish were just made for each other; they were on the same wavelength. They had so many interests in common. Hamish liked dancing and Dad would never do anything like that, he'd always been so reserved. Mum and Hamish liked the same music, the same films, the same holiday destinations . . .

Tom sat in the back seat and felt an awful sinking feeling deep inside, as he realised what she was really telling him. They were leaving Dad. They were leaving Manchester. He knew that he should be shouting about this, telling them to stop the car and let him out, but he was in shock and he could only sit there and listen while his mother prattled on. Hamish had this really fabulous house in a 'sought-after' part of Edinburgh, she told him. He was a widower, his wife had died a couple of years ago and, when he'd met Mum, something had just clicked between them; something incredible, something magical.

'It was like, I don't know, fate or something?' said Mum. She sounded like some love-struck teenager, not like a married woman of thirty-eight. 'We just looked at each other across the room and it was like it was all meant to be, you know what I mean? I thought to myself, Mary, you only get the one chance at happiness and you need to do something about this now, or spend the rest of your life regretting it.'

Through all this, Hamish just sat at the wheel, staring at the road ahead, his eyes narrowed down to slits against the sunlight, an unpleasant smirk on his potato-like face. Occasionally, he lifted one hand from the steering wheel and placed it on Mum's hand and Tom noticed a crude tattoo on his bare arm which read *Scotland Forever*. He didn't look anything like Dad, Tom thought. He looked like an oik, a loser. But Mum just kept on about how wonderful he was, how good he was with kids (he'd raised two of his own; they were grown now, and both of them had responsible jobs), he was a football fan and he'd run a couple of marathons for charity.

Tom finally pulled himself together enough to throw in a couple of objections. What about Mum's job at the catalogue company? What about school?

'Oh, I can walk into another job any time. You know I've always hated working for the catalogue, and as for school, there's a really good comprehensive just a stone's throw from Hamish's house in Fairmilehead, both of his kids went there, we can get you in, no problem! Edinburgh's a fantastic place, it has a castle, seaside, a mountain . . . oh, and the festival every summer! All that stand-up comedy, you'll love that! And listen, you can tell this was meant to be because the school has the same maroon blazers you wear at St Thomas's; all I'll need to do is sew on a new badge!'

'What about my friends?' he pleaded, but she hadn't faltered.

'You'll soon make new ones,' she told him. 'An easygoing lad like you, it'll only take you a few days . . .'

But of course the reality had been so different. From the moment he'd walked into his first class and Mr McKenzie, his form teacher, had introduced him as 'the new arrival,' he'd been a marked man. The other kids spent all their time whispering about him, the 'The Manky,' a blow-in, laughing every time he opened his mouth and spoke in his flat Mancunian accent, imitating him when he was almost, but not quite, out of earshot. He felt like telling them that he hadn't asked to be here, that he hadn't had any say in the matter, but what difference would that have made? He wasn't welcome, simple as that.

And neither did he feel welcome at home. Hamish's 'cool' house had turned out to be a large semi on an anonymous side street of Fairmilehead. It had probably been nice enough once but, after three years of Hamish living there alone, it was looking decidedly scruffy. Whenever Tom was there with Mum and Hamish, he felt as though he was in the way, that they wanted to be alone, so he spent most of his time in his bedroom, the one that had previously belonged to Hamish's eldest son. With its Hibernian F.C. wallpaper and yellowing posters of grinning footballers, it looked as though nobody had been in there for years.

'We'll soon get this decorated more to your taste,' Hamish assured him when he and Mum had first taken him to look at the room. And then he reached out a big hand and tousled Tom's hair. 'I expect you're a United fan, eh?'

Tom had no interest in football whatsoever, and he certainly didn't like Hamish touching him, but he said nothing, just shrugged his shoulders.

'We'll get you a computer,' Mum had added and Hamish had given her an odd look, a kind of a pursed-lip scowl, as if to say 'we'll have to see about that.' When they'd left him to 'make himself at home,' Tom had lain down on the bed and curled himself up into a foetal position, feeling that he wanted to cry, but not allowing himself the comfort of it.

And now, here he was, three weeks later, and he was going on a school trip to something or somewhere called Mary King's Close. When he'd brought the letter home from school, Mum had been keen for Tom to go but Hamish had said that he'd been to it, it was a con, just a trudge along some dirty old streets and not worth the money the school was asking. Mum still hadn't managed to 'walk into' that new job she'd mentioned and Hamish seemed to be watching the pennies. Mum had argued that Tom needed to get out a bit, it would help him make friends, and Hamish said that visiting some old ruin wasn't going to help the kid do that, he needed to stand up for himself a bit more. Right then and there, the couple who were 'so right for each other' had proceeded to have their first row. Tom thought about telling them that he didn't care whether he went or not, but they seemed to have forgotten he was there so he slunk off to his room and left them to it.

Mum must have prevailed though, because the money had been paid and now here was the coach, lurching out of the pouring rain like a giant caterpillar. It came to a halt with a loud hiss of air brakes. Then everyone was piling aboard, pushing and shoving to be first. Tom waited till everyone else was on and then he climbed the steps and trudged along the aisle until he found a seat to himself, as far away as possible from the most vocal of his tormentors, a kid called Stuart Gillies; a big overweight thug of a lad with spiky blonde hair, who took great delight in referring to Tom as 'The Manky'. Gillies was big enough and hard enough to have a small following of admirers who would do just about anything to be in his gang. If slagging off Tom was the price of admission, they were more than willing to join in.

As Tom slid into his seat, he heard Gillies' voice

announcing that, 'The Manky looks like a drowned rat this morning.' This caused some laughter and then another voice, a girl called Jenny, added that it was a pity the Manky's Ma couldn't afford to buy him a coat. 'Oh, they don't wear coats in Manchester,' Gillies assured her. 'Too cool for that.' He adopted a poor Mancunian accent. 'They all think they're Liam bleedin' Gallagher!'

Tom tried to ignore him and stared fixedly out of the window at the rain-lashed street. A tramp in a frayed overcoat was pushing a supermarket trolley piled with his tattered belongings along the pavement, a few wet strands of grey hair plastered to his head. Somehow, he was managing to smoke a roll up, the thin stream of smoke rising between the daggers of rain. Some of the kids at the back of the coach started banging on the window and shouting to him. He looked up and flicked a casual V in their direction with two nicotine-stained fingers.

Mr McKenzie pulled his gangling figure aboard and stood at the front of the coach, doing a quick headcount. He was wearing a camel-coloured duffel coat which somehow made him look like an extra from a movie about World War Two. Then he made an announcement.

'I'd just like to remind everyone that you're representing your school today and we'd like you to act with the necessary decorum.'

This was met with a barrage of groans, laughs and jeers, but he soldiered gamely on.

'Also, don't forget that this is an educational trip, not a holiday. You will each be asked to submit an essay about the Plague of 1645, so I would advise you all to listen attentively to everything you hear today.'

Another long groan. Mr McKenzie gestured to the driver and took a seat at the front of the coach. It pulled away with another hiss of hydraulics and started along the street. Rain streaked diagonally across the window. Tom tried to concentrate his attention on the view but couldn't quite manage to shut out the voices coming from the back of the coach.

'I heard the Manky's mother did a runner on her old man,' said a voice.

'Aye,' agreed Gillies. 'Left him high and dry in Mankyland. Fancied a bit of local talent instead.'

'She's shacked up with Hamish McPherson,' said Jenny. 'I heard my Ma telling her friend.'

'Hamish McPherson. Jesus! She likes to live dangerously. Hamish McPherson with the . . .' The voice lowered to a whisper towards the end of the sentence so Tom couldn't hear what was said, but the derisive laughter at the end suggested that it had been fairly crude.

'Keep it down at the back!' shouted Mr McKenzie and the laughter faded. 'Stuart, don't let me have to tell you again.'

Tom sighed. He wondered what his friends were doing now. In Manchester, he'd have been joining in with the laughter and some other kid would have been the butt of the joke, some spod that everybody made fun of. Here, he was the outsider and it wasn't a nice place to be.

He reached into his pocket and took out his mobile, keeping it well out of sight because school rules didn't allow pupils to have them. It was Pay As You Go, and he was currently out of credit. Mum, sensing perhaps that he would be phoning his dad, had refused point blank to fund the habit, and he'd had to resort to using his dinner money but that only went so far.

The phone had been his lifeline over the past few weeks: he'd texted all his mates back in Manchester, telling them of his woes and, at first, they'd replied to him, expressing their concerns and making vague plans to come up there and rescue him. But, as time went on, they texted less often and now seemed to have given up on him completely. But he'd been texting his dad too and Dad had been texting him back, several times a day and had even phoned him a couple of times.

Dad claimed to have had no inkling about Mum's affair; the first he had known of it was when he got back from work and found the house empty and a letter on the mantelpiece. He had now put the matter in the hands of his solicitors (whatever that meant) and they were trying to find a way that Dad and Tom could be allowed to spend some time together – but the distances involved meant it could take quite a while to do that. In the meantime, Tom was to 'keep his chin up' and work hard at his new school, try to fit in as best he could. The last text Tom had received was an odd one and made him think that his Dad must have been drinking when he wrote it.

Tom. Please remember I will always love you. Dad.

As far as Tom could remember, it was the first time his dad had ever said those words to him.

He sighed and, determined to take his mind off his troubles, he loaded up *Timeslyp* on his phone, a game he'd been playing a lot lately. In it, the hero, John Kane, a lean, craggy man dressed in a wide-brimmed hat and a long leather coat, spent all his time running along endless corridors, dodging attacks from cloaked and masked assassins. They came out of the most unexpected places, leaping through paintings on the wall, oozing up from the bare floorboards beneath Kane's feet, dropping through the ceiling onto his back. He escaped them by performing a series of athletic leaps and somersaults to avoid the razor-sharp sickles they carried. Every so often, Kane would reach a doorway, a portal into another level and, whenever he burst through one of them, he would find himself in an alternate reality, where everything was slightly different and where the rules learned on the previous level no longer applied. It was weirdly addictive. Tom was currently on level six but couldn't quite seem to reach the next doorway. Every time he got close to it, he would be felled by a couple of assassins who jumped out of the shadows, hell-bent on his destruction.

He was so engrossed in the game that it was a complete surprise when the coach, with a great hissing of air brakes, pulled to a halt on the High Street and Mr McKenzie announced that it was time to get off. Tom abandoned the game, noting as he did so that the phone's battery was half gone.

'Great,' he muttered. He shoved the phone into his damp blazer pocket and waited for the other kids to leave the coach before tagging reluctantly along behind them.

Two

The tour started in the gift shop. The class stood around looking at a collection of pencils, fridge magnets, posters and assorted bits of multi-coloured plastic. Tom found himself by a pile of pewter keyrings depicting the tiny figure of a man in a long cloak and a flat-topped hat, carrying a long cane in one hand. He picked one up and took a closer look. Inexplicably, the figure seemed to have the head of a bird, with a long hooked beak and big, goggly eyes.

'Manky's just found a model of his dad,' sneered Gillies, moving past and deliberately jostling Tom with his shoulder. Then he flapped his bent arms up and down and made a clucking sound. Tom dropped the keyring back with the others and stood there, fuming silently, wondering why he felt so unable to stand up to Gillies and the other kids. They were just bullies, after all, and Tom would have had no problem telling them to get lost back in Manchester, but here he felt somehow powerless. So much was wrong with his life right now that he didn't feel able to make the smallest change to anything. But, he thought, how satisfying it would be to turn around and punch Gillies on the nose.

A door set into the wall opened and a young woman came out, dressed in olden-day clothing: a green dress with a white apron and a tightly-fitting cloth cap that drooped down on one side of her head. 'It's Wee Willie Winky!' sniggered Gillies and Mr Mckenzie moved closer to shoot a warning look at him. The woman had obviously heard it all before. She waited calmly until the murmur of conversation had died down and then she performed a curtsy to the waiting children.

'Good morning,' she said. 'My name is Agnes Chambers; I'm a maid and I'll be taking you down to Mary King's Close. Please be very careful on the steps; we don't want any accidents, do we? Now, if you'd like to follow me?'

She turned and led the way through the open door and the class fell into line behind her. Once again, Tom waited till last, well aware how easy it would be for somebody to 'accidentally' barge into him on the steep stone steps that led down into the gloom. The group descended in silence, some of the girls clutching at each other nervously until they found themselves standing at the top of a long run of stone floor, which angled steeply downwards. On either side of them, rough plastered walls, sparsely lit by strategically placed lights, rose up sheer to a dark ceiling high above their heads. Lines hung with ratty looking washing were strung across the gap. 'Agnes' came to a halt and turned to look at the class. She waited for them to gather in front of her.

'You're probably wondering what this place is,' she said. 'What we're looking at here are the streets of the old city, underneath the Royal Mile, just as they would have looked in the 1600's. Well . . . almost. If we'd been down here in the year 1645, we'd have been ankle-deep in raw sewage.'

Tom felt Gillies' elbow jam into his ribs.

'Just like home, eh Manky?' he whispered and there were muted sniggers. Mr McKenzie shushed them to silence and Agnes continued.

'Everywhere, you would have heard the words '*Gardez Loo!*' which was the signal that somebody was about to empty a chamber pot out of a doorway or an upstairs window. You certainly didn't want to be in the way when *that* happened.'

'See,' smirked Gillies, 'What did I tell you? Just like Manchester.'

'The sewage ran downhill from here until it reached the loch, so you can imagine what that must have smelled like.'

'Why don't you tell everyone, Manky?' hissed Gillies. More sniggers.

'In 1753, The Royal Exchange decided to take down the top three floors of Mary King's Close and use the lower ones as foundations for the new City Chambers. So all this was hidden from the public view, locked away until the year 2003, when it was decided to reopen the Close as a tourist attraction. Now, we're going to walk down the hill and look at some of the homes of people who lived here in the 1600's.'

She turned and led them on down the slope.

'Some tourist attraction,' Tom heard Gillies mutter. 'Place looks like it needs a good clean.'

'Yeah, it stinks down here,' agreed one of his cronies. 'Dead borin'.'

But Tom didn't agree. He thought the Close was really atmospheric. In this strange, shadowy world beneath the city, it was all too easy to imagine what it must have been like to live in those times. He pictured the narrow streets filled with the bustle of human life – carts and carriages rattling over the cobbles, salesmen and women shouting out their wares as they wandered through the crowd, ragged children chasing after the carriages to beg for coins.

Now Agnes paused in front of an open doorway and a serious look came to her face. 'We're about to enter the house of one of the Close's residents, John Craig,' she said. 'It's the year 1645, and the bubonic plague has come to the city. When we go into the room, be careful you don't bump in to anybody.'

She led the way in and the group followed. When it came to Tom's turn, he saw that the room was in almost total darkness, save for the light of a lantern beside a roughly made wooden bed. There was a child lying in the bed, his face and bare chest unnaturally pale – and kneeling beside him was a strange and nightmarish figure, similar to the keyring that Tom had looked at earlier. Instead of a hat, he wore a tightly fitting leather helmet, but the face was the same, a great curved beak like a bird of prey and what looked like huge round eyes. It took a few moments to register that the figures were nothing more than waxworks, but it was still an unsettling image.

There was an uncomfortable silence before Jenny said, 'Who's the Crow Man?'

Everybody laughed at this, but Agnes took it all in her stride.

'I've heard him called some interesting names,' she said, 'but that one's a first for me.' She moved closer to the figure. 'This sinister-looking gentleman is Doctor George Rae, Edinburgh's most famous plague doctor, and he's here to treat young Thomas Craig who has contracted bubonic plague, as you can see by the telltale buboes on his body.' She indicated a bright red swelling under the child's left armpit. 'Dr Rae is Edinburgh's second plague doctor. The first, Dr John Paulitious, died in 1645, after just a short time in the job.'

'What did he die of?' asked one boy and his friend gave him a scornful look.

'Work it out,' he said.

Agnes nodded. 'Absolutely,' she said. 'Plague doctoring was a very dangerous profession, but quite lucrative. To take Doctor Paulitious's place, Doctor Rae was promised the incredible salary of one hundred and ten pounds a month. His employers were happy to offer him that because they didn't think he'd live to collect the money, but they were wrong. In the end he had to virtually sue the Town Council for his back pay.'

'But why's he all done up like a big bird?' asked another girl.

Agnes smiled. 'Back in the seventeenth century, people believed that the plague was spread by something called 'miasma' – infected air. The mask that the doctor wore had a beak that was literally stuffed with herbs and flowers, which he thought would act as some kind of filter. He wore goggles to protect his eyes and, of course, his helmet and cloak were made of thick leather.' She studied the class for a moment. 'I wonder if any of you can tell me how the plague was actually spread,' she said.

Before he could stop himself, Tom's hand went up. 'Fleas,' he said.

There was raucous laughter at this, but Agnes soon silenced them with a stern look.

'I don't know why you're laughing,' she told them. 'He's quite right.' She smiled at Tom. 'What else can you tell me?'

'Well...' Tom was aware of Gillies and his mates looking daggers at him, as though The Manky wasn't allowed to know anything about *their* history, but he ignored them and went on. 'The fleas fed on infected rats and then, when the rats died, the fleas moved on to people.'

'Have you been here before?' Agnes asked him, suspiciously.

He shook his head. 'I went to this other place,' he muttered. 'Eyam, in Derbyshire?' He'd been there on a school trip earlier that year. His class had done a project on it and, unlike most projects he'd been involved with, it had been really interesting. They'd got the plague there in the 1660's (he couldn't remember the actual date). The fleas came in on rolls of cloth that a tailor had ordered and near enough the whole village had ended up infected. The villagers were incredibly brave about it and opted to shut themselves off from the rest of the world, forbidding anyone to leave, so they wouldn't spread the sickness. 'I think over two hundred people died there,' he added, 'which was like two-thirds of the village.'

The moment he'd finished talking, Tom regretted it. Gillies was looking at him now with a 'just you wait' expression on his ugly face.

But Agnes smiled. 'That's brilliant,' she said. 'Thanks for

sharing that with us.' She looked around at the children. 'You see, it wasn't just Edinburgh that suffered from the plague; there were outbreaks all over the world. Perhaps the most famous was the Great Plague of London in 1666. I'm sure some of you must have heard of that?' Nobody so much as grunted, so she continued. 'But, going back to our 'Crow Man' here . . .' She flashed a mischievous look at Jenny. 'Although the herbs and flowers in that beak didn't help him one iota, something else about his costume almost certainly saved him from infection. I wonder, would anybody like to hazard a guess about what that might be?'

There was a long, baffled silence, before Tom felt compelled to speak again. 'The leather cloak,' he said. 'The fleas wouldn't have been able to bite through it.'

'Correct!' said Agnes. 'You're certainly on the ball, today.' She looked around at the others. 'Now, if there are no more questions, we'll move on.' She headed for the door and the children shuffled after her. Tom hung back, as ever, but noticed that Gillies was doing the same. The heavyset boy ambled closer until he was standing right beside Tom. He smelled of a mixture of stale sweat and cheese and onion crisps.

'Think you're smart, don't you, Manky?' he murmured.

'Smarter than you, at any rate,' said Tom. His success with the questions must have made him reckless.

'Yeah, you enjoy it while you can. You and me are gonna have a little talk straight after this. We'll see how clever you are, then.'

'Come on, boys, stop hanging around,' said Mr

McKenzie, who was probably already regretting offering to shepherd this outing.

The two boys moved obediently towards the door and Mr McKenzie followed them out. They caught up with the rest of the group just as they came to a halt in front of another doorway.

'The room we are about to go into is in some ways our most famous one,' Agnes told the children. 'Lots of people know the story of it even though they have never visited Mary King's Close. We call it, 'Little Annie's Room,' and, before we go in there, I'm going to tell you the story.' She paused for a moment to make sure she had everyone's attention. 'In the nineteen-nineties, this room was visited by a famous Japanese psychic. She claimed it was the saddest room she had ever visited and that when she stepped inside it, she felt a wee hand pulling at her sleeve . . .'

She paused for effect and some of the more impressionable girls grabbed each other nervously.

'The psychic turned around and saw the ghost of a little girl standing behind her. She was crying. She said her name was Annie and that she was looking for a lost doll. Then she vanished. Well, the psychic was so moved by this experience she went straight out and bought a wee Barbie doll, which she placed in the room in an attempt to cheer Annie up. As I told you, that was some time ago and, over the years in between, visitors to Mary King's Close have added to Annie's collection. Let's go in and have a look, shall we?'

She led the way into the room. Back at the end of the queue, Tom could hear gasps of surprise coming from ahead and, when he finally made it into the room to peer over the rows of heads in front of him, he saw that one corner was piled high with literally hundreds of dolls, teddy bears and cuddly toys of every shape and size.

Agnes continued to talk, but Tom's attention was distracted as somebody moved past the open doorway behind him. He turned his head to look and felt a chill tingling along the length of his spine; he saw that a young girl, perhaps ten or twelve years old, was walking by. She was carrying a straw basket of what looked like vegetables and she was dressed in seventeenth-century clothing: a tattered brown dress and a white cap like Agnes wore, from beneath which a tangle of blonde hair spilled. As she walked by she turned her head to look at Tom and he felt another sense of shock, because she had the most intense blue eyes he had ever seen. But she only looked at him for an instant before turning her head and walking on.

Tom told himself that she was just part of the tour, a young girl dressed as Annie, put there to throw a scare into the visitors to her room, but that didn't seem to make any sense. If that was the case, wouldn't she be positioned somewhere in the room itself, ready to pop out and shout 'Boo!'? As far as Tom could tell, he was the only one who had so much as noticed her. And, if she was just an actress, how had they got that flickery, shimmery quality to her? Some kind of special effect? A projection, something like that?

Against his better judgement, he stepped back from the rest of the group and leaned out to have a look around the edge of the doorway. There was the girl gliding silently along the corridor, seemingly intent on going somewhere. Tom wasn't sure why but he felt impelled to follow. The others were listening to what Agnes was saying and they didn't even notice as he slipped out of the room and went after the girl.

She's not a ghost, he told himself as he walked. *There's a logical explanation for this.*

But he couldn't for the life of him imagine what that might be and he couldn't seem to stop himself from following her just the same.

'Excuse me?' he said and she glanced back at him for a moment, a look of surprise on her face, but then she turned away and increased her pace, as though anxious to get away from him. 'Hey, it's all right, I won't hurt you,' said Tom. 'Hang on a minute!'

There was another doorway up ahead of her, a low opening with a stone lintel across the top of it but it was roped off with a length of thick cord, and prominent signs in bright red letters at either side made it clear that it wasn't a sensible place to go.

DANGER. NO PUBLIC ACCESS BEYOND THIS POINT. KEEP OUT.

Tom had expected the girl to turn away from it, but no, she went straight through the doorway without slowing her pace and, here was the weird thing, she hadn't even bothered to duck under the length of cord that barred the way, but seemed to go through it without disturbing it.

In the heat of the moment, all Tom could think was

that the girl was going into a dangerous place.

'Hey, you!' he shouted. 'Can't you read?'

He quickened his pace in an attempt to catch up with her, but she continued walking into the darkness of the room beyond and, almost without thinking, he jumped over the rope and followed her. As he ducked under the lintel he felt a strange, giddy feeling ripple through him and then found himself walking through almost total darkness, his feet clunking on wooden floorboards. He saw the girl up at the far end of the room, standing in front of an ancient stone fireplace. In the gloom she seemed to flicker and shimmer like a silent movie. Tom took a cautious step forward.

'You really shouldn't be in here,' he told her. 'I don't think it's safe.'

She glanced at him again, her expression one of suspicion, and then she turned her face away from him.

'Look, honestly,' he said, 'I really think it's best if we go outside and I–'

He broke off in alarm as he felt something sag beneath his feet; there was a slow creaking noise, the sound of ancient timbers protesting at his weight. He stayed very still. The girl was looking at him again now, an expression of concern on her face. She turned to face him and he saw with a stab of shock that the front of her dress was stained red with blood.

'OK,' he said. 'I think we'd better–'

And then suddenly, shockingly, everything was falling away beneath him in a slow, grinding roar. He made a desperate attempt to turn back towards the entrance but his feet were no longer standing on anything solid and the next thing he knew, he was falling, falling in the midst of splintered wood and clouds of dust and he seemed to fall for a very long time before he hit the ground.

THREE

He came gradually back to his senses, aware of noise all around him. He was lying face down, his head turned to one side. Something hard was pressing into his right cheek. He opened his eyes and saw a strange tipped-on-one-side world running vertically across his field of vision. He realised that his face was resting on a cobbled street, along which people were moving to and fro in a restless, shouting mass. People in fancy dress, he decided, judging by the many long coats, plumed hats and colourful bonnets he could see. He wanted to move but, for the moment, he felt too nauseous, so he just lay there, blinking, trying to gather his scattered senses. And then he became aware of a noise from somewhere behind him, separating itself from the hubbub all around, a juddering, clattering sound rising steadily in volume as something heavy came thundering towards him.

Realization hit him and he rolled quickly onto his back. Whatever it was raced past, inches from his prone body, metal-clad wheels striking sparks on the cobbles. He tilted his head back and now he was looking upside down at the rear of a carriage moving briskly away from him, pulled by horses that he could hear but couldn't quite see. A scruffy man wearing a weird triangular hat glanced back at him from the driver's seat, an amused grin on his dirty face. He lifted a whip, cracked it in the air and the carriage lurched on along the street.

Now Tom managed to sit upright. He stared around in open-mouthed astonishment. He was still on the Close, he decided, or at least on a wider road that adjoined it, but it all looked different now, packed with human life of every age and description, far too many people to be mere actors and, when he raised his eyes to look for the dark ceiling of the Royal Mile, his astonished gaze found nothing more than a row of high rooftops and above them, a clear blue sky and the sun streaming down into his face. He opened his mouth to say something, but nothing came out. He closed his eyes and then opened them again, hoping that somehow everything would go back to the way it was, but it didn't.

'What's happening?' he asked the world at large but, not surprisingly, he received no answer.

'Are you all right?' The voice made him start. He turned to see the young girl he had been following. She was standing just a short distance from him, one hand on her hip, the other holding her straw basket. She had a quizzical smile on her pretty face and Tom was relieved to see that there was no sign of any blood on her dress. 'You fell over,' she added, just in case he didn't know what had happened to him. 'You said something to me and then you fell.' She had a broad Scottish accent, thick and coarse, unlike any other he had heard since his arrival in Edinburgh.

He sat there blinking at her, trying to find appropriate words but nothing seemed to fit the situation except 'where am I?' and there was no way he was going to say that. So he tried something else. 'The floor gave way,' he muttered.

'Did it?' She looked down at the cobbled street and even tried tapping it with the toe of one boot. 'Seems all right to me,' she said.

'Not *this* floor, stupid. The other one: the wooden one in the room where you weren't supposed to go.'

She studied him warily as though she suspected he was some kind of lunatic. 'I wouldn't sit there if I was you,' she said. 'For one thing, it's very dirty. And for another . . .'

As if to illustrate her point, a second carriage came rattling towards Tom from the opposite direction, the horses wild-eyed and snorting as the driver urged them onwards with no concern for the confused-looking boy sitting in the middle of the road. Tom took the hint. He scrambled to his feet and dodged aside, then watched in amazement as the vehicle rattled past. Through an open window there was a glimpse of a man in a powdered white wig and a fancy gold jacket. He was staring expressionlessly out at the world but he grinned when he saw Tom, revealing twin rows of rotten green teeth.

'What the . . . what *is* this?'

Tom turned to speak to the girl again and saw that she was moving off the main road and along a crowded narrow side street, as though she had dismissed him completely. He felt a sense of panic rising within him so he hurried after her into the Close, where tenement buildings reared up on either side of him, seven or eight storeys high. He didn't have the first idea what was happening and he hoped she might be able to explain it to him.

'Annie!' he shouted. 'Hold on a bit, wait for me.'

She paused and directed a baffled look at him. 'Annie?' she echoed. 'I think you have the wrong girl. I'm Morag.'

'Oh, uh . . . OK. She said your name was Annie.'

'Who said?'

'The woman from Mary King's Close. Agnes. Agnes Chambers?'

'I don't know anybody on the Close by that name.' Morag started to move away again. 'I have to get going,' she said. 'You'll make me late and then there'll be trouble.'

'I'll come with you,' he said. He fell into step beside her and they walked on along the crowded street, having to push their way through the heaving mass of human traffic, while he tried to put everything together in his mind, so he could make some kind of sense of it. OK, so he'd had a fall. That much he was sure of. Chances were he was lying unconscious somewhere and all this . . . he stared in wide-eyed amazement at his surroundings in all their incredible complexity – all *this* was probably some kind of dream he was having while they fixed him up. He couldn't help thinking about Kane, the hero of *Timeslyp*, bursting through a doorway to find himself in an unfamiliar world. Maybe that idea had somehow wormed its way into his mind.

Either that or he'd time-travelled back to the seventeenth century. And there was no way that could have happened. Was there?

Meanwhile, it was hard to concentrate, because at every few steps there was some amazing new thing to grab his attention. Here, in the entrance to what must have been a butcher's shop, a pig was strung up by its back legs and a couple of men were removing its guts and heaping them into a series of metal buckets. Blood slopped over the edges and ran down the centre of the already filthy street. There, out on the cobbles, a man with a soaped-up face was sitting in a barber's chair while another man wearing a white wig shaved him with a cut-throat razor.

'Gardez Loo!' shouted a voice from up above and an instant later a bucket of foul-smelling slops hurtled down from a balcony and struck the cobbled street, splashing in all directions. An old man who had failed to step back in time shook his fist at the woman who had emptied the bucket, an odd-looking creature with a white painted face and rouged cheeks. She was leaning over the balcony and laughing openly at his predicament, displaying quite a bit of cleavage as she did so. Tom tried not to stare. He moved on, taking more notice of where he was walking and he saw that, though the sewage was mostly dry and baked by the sun, a sluggish trickle of wet stuff still coursed its way along the middle of the street and his shoes were already plastered with evil-smelling muck. Mum was going to be delighted when he got home. *If* he got home . . .

'Where are we going?' he asked Morag and she shot him a funny look.

'*I'm* going to Missie Grierson's,' she said. 'I don't know where *you're* going.'

'I'm . . . I'm going there too,' he told her, quickly.

'Why? Are you an orphan?' she asked him.

He thought for a moment. 'Yeah,' he said. 'Sure. Sort of.'

'How can you be 'sort of' an orphan?' she asked him. She didn't get an answer so she went on. 'You talk funny,' she observed. 'You dress funny too. What's that red coat you're wearing?'

'It's just a school uniform,' said Tom defensively.

'You go to *school*?' Morag seemed impressed at this.

'Sure. Doesn't everyone?'

Morag laughed, as though he'd made a joke, but he couldn't see anything remotely funny about what he'd said. 'And the voice?' she prompted him.

'Oh, I'm from Manchester.' She looked at him blankly as though he'd said he was from Mars. 'You've heard of Manchester, right?' He tried to think of something that might be familiar to her. 'Manchester United?' he ventured. 'You know, the football team?'

He might as well have been talking in a foreign language.

'Are you a *Sassenach*?' she asked him and he frowned, nodded. He was pretty sure he knew what that word meant. A blow-in. An outsider. The kids at his school didn't use the word, but it was how they saw him.

Now Tom and Morag were pushing their way through some kind of outdoor market, grubby little wooden buildings with thatched roofs, where men and women stood shouting at the passers-by to come and taste their produce. 'Mutton pie!' one man was shouting. 'Finest in Edinburgh, who'll try my wares?' But nobody seemed interested in pies today. 'Fresh fruit!' shouted an odd-looking woman with a painted face and very few teeth. Like her, the apples and pears piled up on her stall looked well past their best.

'Missie Grierson says you should never trust a

Sassenach,' said Morag, brightly. 'She says as how they're all thieves and rascals.'

'Not me,' Tom assured her. 'And what does this Missie Grierson know about it anyway?'

'Plenty,' Morag assured him. 'She's the wisest person on the Close. When a woman's due to have a bairn, she's the first one they come looking for. Missie Grierson says if she'd been around when I was born, then maybe my mother would still be here to look after me.'

'Your mother?' Tom didn't quite understand what she was saying. 'Why, where is your mother?' he asked.

'In heaven, with the angels, silly. When I came into the world, she had to leave. Missie Grierson says the angels wanted her because she was so pretty.' Her pale face grew very serious. 'I spoke to an old woman who was there that night. She said there was a lot of blood.' She seemed to dismiss the idea. 'But Missie Grierson took me in and looked after me and now I work at the orphanage.' She made a smile that was a little too forced. 'She's been very kind.'

'You *work*?' Tom stared at her. 'But . . . you can't be more than, what? Ten or twelve? Shouldn't you be in school?'

'Oh aye, and I should be the Queen of Scotland, while I'm at it.' She looked thoughtful. 'So what happened to *your* parents?' she asked unexpectedly.

'Er . . . they split up,' said Tom. 'Dad stayed back in Manchester and Mum . . . well, she moved up here to Edinburgh.'

'So you're not really an orphan at all!' cried Morag, sounding outraged.

'I kind of am,' he insisted. 'And anyway, I'm . . . lost.'

'Well, I wouldn't get your hopes up,' Morag warned him. 'Missie Grierson is not one to be . . . oh!'

Morag had suddenly spotted something up ahead and instinctively she stepped to the side of the street, grabbing Tom's sleeve and pulling him with her. He glanced down at her and saw that she was averting her eyes from whatever she had seen. He looked along the street and felt a shock go through him. A figure was striding towards them, a man dressed in an outlandish but strangely familiar costume. His leather cloak billowed out behind him and his weird goggle eyes, set either side of the long, curved beak, stared at the world like those of some alien being. In one gloved hand he carried a long stick and Tom saw that he was using it to prod and push people out of his way, as though they were no more than cattle. His heavy boots rang out on the cobbles.

As the man moved past, his head turned to look in Tom's direction and Tom felt his blood run cold as those hideous goggle-eyes came to rest on him. It was only for an instant, but Tom imagined that he could feel their gaze burning into him, looking deep within him as if to capture his innermost secrets. Then the boots rang on stone again and the cloaked figure swept past and continued on his way.

Morag seemed to remember to breathe. She stepped back to the middle of the path and continued walking. Tom had to run a couple of steps to catch her up.

'That was Doctor Rae, wasn't it?' he said.

She nodded but seemed reluctant to speak.

'The Plague Doctor?' insisted Tom.

Again she nodded but kept her gaze on the way ahead as though she didn't want to encourage him.

'Amazing,' he murmured.

Morag glanced up at him. 'What is?' she asked.

'I saw him before. Well, not him, really, but a waxwork that was meant to be him. You know, a waxwork?' Again, that blank look. 'It's kind of like a pretend person,' he explained. 'Anyway, he looked just the same . . .' He thought for a moment. Whether this was a dream or a hallucination, he might as well play along with it. 'What year is this?' he asked.

Morag managed a smile. 'How would I know?' she asked him.

'You don't know what *year* it is?' He stared at her in disbelief.

Morag shrugged. 'It's sixteen forty-something, I think.'

'Sixteen forty-five,' he said. He glanced up at the clear blue sky overhead. 'Summer. And . . . I'll bet there's plague here, right?'

Morag nodded. 'Every day it gets worse,' she said. 'Doctor Rae is new, only been around a week or so. We had Doctor Paulitious before him and everyone said he was a good man; he just wanted to help the sick people. But he got sick himself and died a horrible death. And this Rae fellow . . .' She shook her head. 'There are many who say he is just out to line his own nest.'

Tom looked at her. 'Meaning?'

'He's being paid a lot of money.'

'Oh yeah, I heard about that.'

'People say that he'll die soon, anyway.'

'He won't,' said Tom, and Morag gave him an inquiring look.

'How would you know that?' she asked him.

'It's just a . . . hunch.'

'Hmm. Well, anyway, here we are.'

'Huh?'

Morag had come to a halt in front of a dark timber doorway, above which a crudely painted wooden sign hung. On it was scrawled one word:

ORFENAGE

Tom gazed up at it and shook his head. 'Somebody can't spell,' he observed, pointing at the sign.

Morag looked up at it blankly.

'It should be spelt with a P-H,' he explained and, once again, she gave him an odd look.

'How would you know that?' she asked him.

'It's easy,' he said. O-R-P-H . . .'

'I don't have the book-learning,' she interrupted him flatly. She gestured to the door. 'Anyway, I'm going in now. If you want to talk to Missie Grierson, I can take you to her. But I warn you, she doesn't suffer fools for long. It's up to you.'

Tom considered for a moment. He was completely lost here, out of his element, and Morag was the one person who connected him to the world he had just left. It seemed to him that, as long as he was stuck here, he had little choice but to go with the flow and see what happened.

'I'll come in with you,' he said.

'Suit yourself,' said Morag. She opened the door and led him inside.

FOUR

They were in a long, badly-lit corridor that smelled of cabbage and something much worse that Tom couldn't identify. A rickety-looking staircase rose up on their right, but Morag led the way straight ahead, clearly knowing exactly where she was going. Tom stumbled along behind her, hoping that, in a moment or two, something would happen, there'd be a sudden flash or a puff of smoke and he'd find himself back in more familiar territory. But, annoyingly, everything stayed just the way it was – dark, smelly and forbidding.

Morag pushed through a wooden doorway and led Tom into a big kitchen where two ragged children were at work. A lanky ginger-haired boy was peeling a mountain of vegetables stacked on a surface beside him and a skinny dark-haired girl was pushing a filthy-looking mop across an equally filthy floor, rearranging the dirt. They both looked as though they wouldn't dare to pause for breath.

Standing in front of a huge black cooking range was a middle-aged woman that Tom instantly knew had to be Missie Grierson. She was big and heavyset, her ample curves encased in a grubby black dress that seemed to be quite literally coming apart at the seams. It wasn't that she was fat but rather, very muscular for a woman. She had shoulders and arms that would not have disgraced a champion weightlifter and, as a result, her head looked somehow too small for her body. It was covered by an odd little frilly hat and from her mouth jutted a white clay pipe that was puffing out great clouds of fragrant smoke. Her steely grey eyes were flicking restlessly around the kitchen while she uttered terse instructions to the children all around her.

'Come along, Cameron, it would be nice to have the soup on the boil some time this century! Alison, put more effort into that mopping; I want to see ma face in it when you've finished. Ach, girl, you'll no' get anywhere like that; use a bit of elbow grease, for goodness sake!' She noticed Morag's approach and gave her a long-suffering look. 'Oh, you're back at last; I thought perhaps you'd left the country.' She pulled the pipe from her mouth and poked the stem of it amongst the sorry collection of vegetables in the girl's basket. 'Is this the best you could get?' she muttered. 'It all looks worm-eaten. It's barely fit for the pigs.'

Morag nodded. 'Mr Hamilton said he'll no' give us anything better until you've settled his account in full,' she explained.

'Is that a fact?' Missie Grierson looked annoyed. 'The brass neck of that man! He knows I'm good for it; why must he vex me like this? You gave him the two shillings towards what we owe him?'

'Aye. He made me drop it into a cup of vinegar and he counted to ten before he took it out again. He said it was protection against the contagion.'

'Is that right?' Missie Grierson grunted. 'Where do they get these notions?' she muttered. She noticed Tom for the first time and returned her pipe to her mouth while she studied him in detail. She didn't seem to care much for what she was looking at. 'What've we got here?' she asked doubtfully.

'Oh, this is . . .' Morag stared at Tom blankly. 'I don't believe you told me your name,' she said.

'It's Tom. Tom Afflick.' Tom held out his hand to shake, as he'd been taught to do when first meeting somebody, but Missie Grierson just looked at the hand, as though it wasn't clean enough for her liking. 'What've I told you about bringing home waifs and strays?' she snarled at Morag. 'Even ones dressed in fancy red jackets.'

'I didn't bring him,' protested Morag. 'He followed me.'

'Did he indeed?' Missie Grierson returned her attention to Tom. 'If you're selling something, I'm not interested – unless, of course, it's tobacco. I can always use tobacco.'

'I'm not selling anything,' Tom assured her.

'In that case, I'll not detain ye a moment longer. Kindly close the door on your way out.'

There was a silence then, while Tom stood there unsure of what to do. He looked at Morag, seeking support and, after a pause she spoke up on his behalf.

'But, Missie Grierson, Tom tells me he's a sort of orphan.'

'Is that so?' Missie Grierson studied Tom with a 'seen it all before' expression on her ruddy face. 'What's a 'sort-of' orphan exactly?'

Tom frowned. 'It's complicated,' he said.

'Try me,' suggested Missie Grierson. 'Would that be you've 'sort of' got parents and you've 'sort of' got a home? That kind of thing?'

'Well . . .' Tom racked his brains to try and think of something he might say that didn't sound crazy but in the end, decided he had no option but to tell the truth. 'See, I was on this school trip to Mary King's Close . . .'

'You go to school?' interrupted Missie Grierson. She seemed suddenly a lot more interested.

'Er . . . yes, of course,' said Tom.

'Does that mean you can read?'

Tom shrugged. 'Sure,' he said.

'Wait right there!' Missie Grierson turned away and hurried over to a wooden dresser, the shelves of which were literally stuffed with heaps of paper. She poked frantically through them until she found what she was looking for, then pulled out a single sheet and brought it back over to Tom. She shoved it into his hands. 'Read that,' she demanded. 'Aloud.'

Tom uncrumpled the thick, roughly textured paper. He saw that it was covered with fancy old-fashioned handwriting, the kind that would have been written with a quill pen. He studied it for a moment. Some of the spelling was distinctly odd and the hand was very ornate but he thought he could just about make sense of it.

'Well, go on,' said Missie Grierson impatiently. 'I thought you said you could read.'

'I can. It's just the handwriting is a bit funny. Hasn't this guy ever heard of a compu . . .' He tailed off as he realised what he had been about to say. 'Anyway, it goes something like this.' He began to read haltingly and was aware as he did so, that everybody in the room had stopped work and was gazing at him with what could only be described as utter amazement.

Dear Mistress Grierson,

The Trust has . . . considered your recent request for financial help with the . . . running of your orphanage and, after some . . . discussion, I regret to inform you that we cannot undertake to offer you our help in this matter. We trust you will . . . understand and respect our decision and, of course, we . . . wish you every success with your future enterprise.

Yours sincerely,

Lord Kelvin
President

There was a long silence and then Missie Grierson pulled the pipe from her lips and spat on the floor, narrowly missing Tom's feet.

'It's just as I expected,' she announced to the room in general. She looked around at the children in the kitchen. 'Nobody cares about you but me. What's going to happen to you after I'm gone? That's anybody's guess. Still, at least this time it hasn't cost me a shilling to be told such dismal news.' She considered for a moment and then asked them, 'Why have you stopped working? I don't recall anybody telling you to take a break.'

The children fell back to their respective chores as though their very lives depended on it and Missie Grierson turned her attention back to Tom.

'Where did you learn to read like that?' she asked him.

'At school,' he told her, matter-of-factly. 'It's no big deal.'

'Hmmph.' She rubbed her gnarled chin between a plump thumb and forefinger. 'A rich man's son, I'm guessing . . . and a *Sassenach*, judging by your accent. I've always maintained that Sassenachs are all . . .'

'Thieves and rascals,' finished Tom. 'Yeah, Morag told me. But I'm no thief and I'm not even sure what a rascal is.'

She seemed amused by this remark. 'I'd say you fit the description well enough,' she observed. 'So what happened to your parents?'

'They . . . they're a long way away now,' he said, with what felt like absolute truthfulness. 'My dad is back in Manchester and my Mum . . . well, she's in a different place altogether.'

Missie Grierson clearly misunderstood the last part. A sad look came to her grizzled face. 'I'm very sorry for your loss,' she said. 'Wherever she is, I'm sure the angels are with her.'

Not in Fairmilehead, thought Tom, but he said nothing.

'And there's no way you can get back to your father?'

Tom shook his head. If things didn't go back to the way they were before the fall, he wouldn't be seeing any familiar faces.

'Well, I'll admit that having somebody who can read letters would be handy enough,' admitted Missie Grierson. 'But the need doesn't arise that often. And look around you, laddie; I already have three mouths to feed and it doesn't get any easier.'

'Couldn't he take wee Davey's place?' asked Morag.

There was a deep silence after this was said. Tom

glanced nervously around the room to see that the other children had stopped working and bowed their heads as though disturbed by the very mention of the boy's name.

'Who's wee Davey?' he asked.

'Ach, he was just a boy who was here before,' said Morag. She sounded evasive. 'We all loved wee Davey. He made us laugh.'

'What happened to him?'

'He . . . well, he died.'

'Oh.' Tom frowned. 'Was it the plague?' he asked.

'No it was not!' snapped Missie Grierson, leaning forward to glare at him. 'It was the consumption, everyone knows that. We've no plague here.'

'But I thought . . .'

'Oh aye, there's plague in the Close, sure enough; you'll see the white sheets hanging in the windows and some of them not so very far from here. But with wee Davey it was the consumption, and don't you be telling anyone any different, d'you hear me?'

Tom nodded. 'Sure, I was only . . .'

'The thing about wee Davey, as you'll have guessed by his name, he was only small but he was strong too. He could carry sacks full of potatoes without breaking a sweat. Could you do that?'

'Well,' said Tom. 'I *suppose* I could. I've never really had much call to do it. Tesco always delivered ours.'

'Tess who?'

'Never mind,' said Tom. He reminded himself that he really should think before he opened his big mouth. 'I'm pretty strong,' he said, trying to change the subject. 'I played rugby at my last school.' He saw the blank look on her face and corrected himself. 'I played *sports!*' He bunched his hands into fists and lifted his arms, strongman style. 'Check them out,' he offered.

'I'll take your word for it.' Missie Grierson puffed on her pipe a bit more and then seemed to come to a decision. 'I suppose we can try you out, see if you measure up. But let me warn you, any slacking and you'll be out on your backside; there's no room for that sort here. We all pitch in, isn't that right, children?'

'Aye!' came back the reply, as though they'd rehearsed it.

'So, do you think you could fit in with us?' asked Missie Grierson.

'I'll give it my best shot,' said Tom.

Morag couldn't seem to stop smiling. 'Shall I show him where he'll be sleeping?' she asked.

'No you will not! The very idea!' Missie Grierson crooked a finger at the red-headed boy. 'Cameron, you take a break from that peeling and let Morag earn her supper for a change. Then you take Tom upstairs and show him his bed.' She looked at Tom. 'Where are your bags?' she asked him.

'I haven't got any,' he told her.

'Oh, come along now, you must have a knapsack or something? A cloth bundle, maybe. Everybody has to carry *something* with them.'

Tom shook his head. 'I . . . left in kind of a hurry,' he said.

She gave him a suspicious look. 'Oh, hang on a minute.

You're no' in trouble with the constables, are ye?'

'Oh no,' he assured her. 'Nothing like that.'

'I hope not, because if I find out that there's something you haven't told me, there will be trouble, of that I can promise you.'

Tom ran it through in his mind. *Well, actually, Missie G. there is something I haven't mentioned. You see, I'm from the 21st century and I've ended up here and I've no idea how it happened or how I'm ever going to get back . . .*

But she was already gesturing to him to get moving, so he followed the lanky red-headed lad towards the door through which he had first entered the kitchen. Behind him, he heard Missie Grierson giving orders again.

'Right, you lot, that's enough standing around for one day, get to work! Morag, put down that basket, stop gawping like a fish out of water and start peeling those tatties. I don't know about you lot, but I am starving!'

Her words were the last thing he heard as the door closed behind him and he followed the boy called Cameron along the entrance hall and up a dark and rickety staircase.

FIVE

Cameron led Tom up seven flights of stairs. At each landing, the stairs angled back on themselves to rise to the next floor and it was apparent that other people were living up on these levels. Tom could hear the sounds of conversation coming from open doorways and, on one level, he caught the smell of pipe tobacco. On the fourth floor, a fat man in a long, curly wig came out of a doorway and nodded to Cameron.

'You, boy,' he said. 'I need the services of a pot clenger.'

'Very good, Mr Selkirk. I'll be right on to it in a moment,' Cameron assured him. 'I just have to show Tom his sleeping quarters first.'

The man studied Tom for a moment. 'New boy, eh?' he said.

Tom nodded.

'Well, make sure you work hard and keep your fingers out of other folks' belongings and you and I will get along fine.' He smiled and strolled back along the landing. Cameron led the way upwards again.

Tom gave Cameron a quizzical look.

'Who's he?' he asked.

'Just one of the neighbours,' said Cameron, as though it was of no importance.

'And what did he mean, he needs a *pot . . .?*'

'*Clenger*. He means he wants me to empty his chamber pot.'

Tom stared at him. 'And you . . . you don't mind doing that?' he asked, horrified.

'Mind it? Of course not. He'll pay me a penny for my trouble.' Cameron nodded towards the next flight of stairs. 'We sleep up top,' he said.

Eventually they came to a small, dingy room under the cobweb-festooned eaves of the house. It was empty, save for a rough-looking bed. Tom gazed at it doubtfully. The bedding looked grubby and verminous, not what he was used to at all – but, he told himself, at least there weren't any Hibernian posters blu-tacked onto the rough-plastered walls.

'That's where you'll sleep,' said Cameron. His accent was thicker and more impenetrable than Morag's. He had a long thin face and bright blue eyes. Scatterings of brown freckles were smeared across the bridge of his nose.

'You don't snore, do you?' he asked.

'I don't think so,' said Tom.

'Good. Wee Davey used to snore something terrible. I'd lie there some nights thinking I'd never get to sleep.'

'Is that why you killed him?' It had been meant as a joke but Cameron didn't seem to see the funny side of it.

'I never killed nobody,' he protested. 'And don't you go saying that I did!'

'Hey, chill,' Tom advised him. 'It was just a joke.'

'A joke, is it? I don't think it's very funny.'

'Er . . . all right, sorry.' Tom looked hopefully around the room. 'So . . . where's your bed?' he asked.

Cameron pointed. 'There,' he said.

Tom stared for a moment. 'But . . . you just said that one's mine.'

Cameron rolled his eyes. 'Aye, that's where we *both* sleep. Why d'you think I asked if you snore?'

Tom was horrified. 'We sleep in the same bed? But I counted three of you down in the kitchen . . .'

'The girls have their own room,' said Cameron, looking appalled. 'We sleep up here.'

'Well, I don't much care for that idea,' said Tom. 'I'm used to having my own space.'

'Lucky old you,' said Cameron. 'But beggars can't be choosers, can they?'

'I suppose not,' admitted Tom. He went over to the bed and sat down gingerly on the grimy covers. 'So, what's the deal here?' he asked. 'I mean, how does it work with Missie Grierson and everything?'

Cameron turned to look at Tom. 'She feeds us and gives us a roof over our heads. In return, we work for her.' He shrugged his narrow shoulders. 'She takes in laundry and we help to wash it. We do odd jobs for the neighbours, emptying chamber pots, fetching and carrying, whatever earns a penny.'

'And you're all orphans, right?'

Cameron nodded. 'Aye.' He came and sat on the other side of the bed. 'Did I hear you right just now? Your father is still alive in England?'

'Er . . . yeah. At least, I think so.'

'So why don't you just make your way back to him?'

'It's not as easy as that,' Tom assured him.

'Let me tell you, if my Ma or Da were still alive, I'd get to them no matter what it took,' said Cameron scornfully.

'Yeah? Well, respect to that. But you don't understand. It's more complicated than you think.'

'How so?'

'Well, OK, since you ask . . .' Tom took a deep breath. 'I'm actually from the 21st century . . . that's like about five hundred years from now. I came to visit the Close with a bunch of other kids from my school, but it wasn't like it is now; it was sort of the remains of it, all buried under these new buildings, the way it's going to look in five hundred years' time.'

'Uh huh,' said Cameron. His face was expressionless.

'And I saw Morag there, but not like she really is; she was sort of all flickery and that, like an old movie?' He thought for a moment, realising that this wouldn't mean anything to Cameron. 'Like a ghost, you know? And I thought she was this other girl, Annie, that was supposed to have died here, so I followed her into this room where I wasn't supposed to go and the floor gave way under me and when I woke up, I . . .' Tom's voice trailed away.

Cameron was just sitting there, looking blankly back at him. It wasn't that he was thinking Tom was a nutcase or anything, it was just that what he had heard meant absolutely nothing to him. Tom might as well have been talking in Chinese.

There was a long silence then Cameron stood up and said, 'Well, I've shown ye the bed. I'd better get down and see to Mr Selkirk's chamber pot, before he gives that penny to somebody else. I wouldn't hang around up here too long if I was you, because Missie Grierson will have work for you too. There's always work.'

And, with that, he turned away and went back down the stairs.

'Great,' muttered Tom. 'Now I've got a job.' He sat and stared resentfully after Cameron for several minutes, wondering what on earth he was supposed to do now. He looked around the grubby room and then announced aloud, 'If you want to put everything back the way it was, that's all right with me.' He had no idea who he was supposed to be talking to, but whoever it was didn't bother to give any kind of answer. 'This is nuts,' he said and, just in case there should be any doubt, he said it again for good measure. 'This is NUTS!'

A thought occurred to him and he reached into his blazer pocket and pulled out his mobile. He pressed the 'on' button and looked hopefully at the screen but he wasn't really surprised to see a 'No service' message. He could hardly have hoped to find anything resembling a phone signal in the seventeenth century when he sometimes had enough trouble getting one in the twenty-first.

He sighed and turned out his pockets. He found a crumpled five pound note, which he'd been given in order to buy some lunch, a few assorted coins, a key to his parents' house in Manchester (Hamish hadn't gotten around to giving him a key for the house in Fairmilehead yet), a grubby paper tissue, and a cardboard box containing two blister packs of antibiotic pills. He'd forgotten he had them; they'd been prescribed months ago for a suspected ear infection, which had cleared up the moment he'd started taking them, so only two pills were missing. They'd been in his pocket ever since. Typically, Mum hadn't even bothered to check the pockets when she'd sewn the new school badge on. He put them down with the other things and stared at them dismally, telling himself that this was all he had left in the world and none of it was any use to him – he wouldn't even be able to spend the money. He gave a grunt of disgust and crammed the items back into his pocket.

Just then, his attention was caught by a sudden scuffling noise in the far corner of the room. He turned his head to look and was horrified to see a sleek grey shape scuttling along the base of the wall. A rat, bigger than he could ever have imagined. He suppressed a shudder and got quickly up from the bed. He'd never been fond of rats, even though his experience of them had mostly been confined to films he'd seen and horror stories he'd read. This one was for real and, frankly, way too close for comfort. Without hesitation, he hurried across the room to the staircase and went down, three steps at a time.

Six

In the kitchen, Missie Grierson was still issuing instructions to her orphan workforce. When Tom came in, she studied him doubtfully.

'Settled in, are ye?' she asked him.

'Not really,' he told her. 'You've got rats up there.'

This remark seemed to puzzle her. 'So?' she murmured.

'Well, I'm not being funny, but . . . that's not right, is it? Rats . . . in a bedroom. That's mingin'.'

Now she took her pipe from her mouth and gave an odd snickering laugh.

'And how would you propose I keep them out?' she asked. 'Send them a strongly worded letter? Rats is rats, son. They go wherever they've a mind to.'

'Yeah, but you need to get rid of 'em! What about all the plague that's around the Close? Don't you know that rats spread it?'

Now she looked quite bewildered and Tom realised why. Seventeenth-century people would have had no idea about the causes of bubonic plague. What was it that Agnes Chambers had told the class? They believed it was spread by a miasma – bad air – which was why Doctor Rae always wore that mask, the beak of which was stuffed with flowers and herbs.

'I never heard tell of such a thing,' said Missie Grierson.

'Rats are everywhere. If *they* spread the plague, then the good Lord help us all.'

'It's not just the rats,' Tom assured her. 'It's the fleas, too.'

'The fleas?'

'Yes. The fleas feed on the rats and then they bite the people and . . .' He broke off at the sounds of laughter from behind him and he saw that Morag and Alison were chuckling as though he'd just told a joke. 'It's not funny,' he protested. 'It's what really happens. It's how plague is caused.'

'The fleas bite the rats!' sang Alison.

'The rats bite the people!' joined in Morag.

'We all fall down!' added Alison.

Tom glared at them and their laughter faded away.

'I'm being deadly serious,' he told them. 'It's not meant to be funny.'

Missie Grierson seemed to dismiss the matter. 'I've no doubt there's lots of strange ideas being bandied about across the border,' she said. 'And who am I to say that there isn't something in it? But like I say, rats is rats; you'll no' keep them out of anywhere they want to go and that's a fact.'

The door swung open and Cameron entered, carrying a full chamber pot from which issued an unbelievable stench.

'Auld Mr Selkirk's been eating cheese again,' he announced and Morag and Alison groaned, as though this were a regular occurrence.

'What are you going to do with that?' Tom asked in disbelief as Cameron hurried past.

The boy gave him a scornful look. 'What do you suppose I'm going to do with it?' he smirked. 'I'm going to take it outside and beat it to death with a stick.'

'You *will* wash your hands after you've finished, won't you?' Tom called after him.

'Why would I want to do that?' muttered Cameron, as he passed through another door.

Tom turned to look at Missie Grierson. 'You must make him wash his hands,' he told her. He gestured around at the other kids. 'All of them. If they handle . . . poo, they've got to scrub their hands with soap and hot water.'

'Another of your strange Sassenach customs?' she asked him. 'I wouldn't worry. They'll all be doing the laundry in a while and there's plenty of soap and hot water to be had there.'

'Yes, but they're working with food *now!*'

Missie Grierson waved away his worries and gave him an inquiring look.

'Don't make me regret giving you a chance,' she advised him. 'Now, I've been thinking about how we might make best use of you around here. How are you with pigs?'

Tom actually took a step back in surprise. 'Pigs?' he echoed. 'You mean like . . . *real* pigs?'

'No, I mean straw ones,' said Missie Grierson and, when he seemed to relax a little, she added, 'Of course, real pigs, do you know of any other kind? What experience have you with 'em?'

'Well, I'm fond of a bacon sandwich,' said Tom. 'If that helps?'

Missie Grierson shook her head. 'I mean, have you

looked after them?' she cried.

'I don't think I've ever seen one until today,' he admitted. 'And that one was dead. Before that, I've only seen them in photographs.'

'In where?'

'I mean, like . . . in pictures?'

This caused even more merriment among the orphans.

'He's never seen a pig!' echoed Alison gleefully, 'Except in pictures!'

'Well, I'm from the city,' argued Tom. 'You don't get pigs in the city, do you? You only ever see them out in the . . .' His voice trailed away. 'Oh right, this *is* a city . . . and . . . somebody was chopping up a pig on the way here, so . . . I suppose you *do* have them, right?'

'Of course!' cried Morag. 'The best porkers on the Close!'

'Ask anybody,' said Alison proudly. 'You haven't tasted pork until you've tried some of ours. The secret's in what we feed them.'

Missie Grierson waved to silence her. 'Too much jibber-jabber,' she said. 'Morag, show Tom where he'll be working. And mind you don't stay out there all day. We need to make a start on the laundry.'

The girl nodded, wiped her hands on her apron and then, stepping away from the sink, she stooped and picked up a big iron bucket filled with potato peelings and other scraps of thrown-away food. She swung her head to indicate that Tom should follow her and led him across the kitchen to a door, which she barged open with one shoulder to reveal a small, sun-blasted yard at the back of the house. She stepped outside and Tom followed – then almost reeled backwards as the smell hit him full in the face.

'There,' said Morag, grinning. 'Here are our lovely ladies, all ready to meet you.' Several huge pink shapes were waddling around in the mud-filled yard, snuffling and grunting contentedly. Morag started pointing to the pigs, identifying each of them in turn. 'That one's Bessie, she's my favourite; she's so wise she can almost talk to you. That one with the black ear, that's Mary; you need to watch her 'cos she can be a bit of a handful. The one with all the wee bairns around her is Matilda and . . . Tom, whatever's wrong with you?'

He was hunched over, desperately trying not to heave. The smell was unbelievable, quite the most disgusting stench he had ever encountered, and he was almost afraid to breathe because it felt as though the foul air was burning his lungs. He turned to head back through the doorway in to the house but Morag caught his sleeve and pulled him further into the yard.

'Ach, come on with ye!' she chided him.

'I can't!' gasped Tom. 'What about the awful smell?'

Morag grinned mischievously. 'Oh, don't worry, they'll soon get used to it!' She laughed delightedly at his outraged expression. 'Come on, it's no' that bad.'

'It's 'orrible,' snorted Tom. He had pulled a grubby tissue from his pocket and was holding it over his mouth and nose. 'How can you stand it?'

'You'll soon get used to it. Goodness, you Sassenachs must lead an odd kind of life, if you've never smelled pigs.

Here . . .' She set down the bucket of slops. 'Perhaps you'd like to feed 'em?' She indicated an empty trough on the far side of the yard. 'Just dump it all in there,' she suggested.

Tom looked for a clear path to the trough but soon realised there wasn't one. It meant wading through an ankle-deep slurry of mud and excrement to reach it. 'These are my school shoes,' he protested.

Morag looked down at her battered old boots. 'These are my *only* ones, but there's just the one way to get to that trough, unless you know how to fly. Go on with ye and stop acting like a baby.'

He picked up the bucket and began to wade grimly over to the trough. His feet sank to the ankles, the thick glop tugging at them, threatening to pull his shoes right off. Every time he lifted a leg, a fresh wave of the stench flowed around him and he could feel his eyes filling with moisture. To make matters worse, the pigs were clearly aware of the reason for his visit and they came charging over to him to root at the bucket, their great bristling bodies jostling him, nearly knocking him over.

'Don't lose your footing,' Morag shouted helpfully. 'Pigs will eat anything they find on the ground.'

'Thanks for the advice,' he muttered. He made it to the trough and upended the bucket of slops into it. He was instantly surrounded by a crowd of grunting pigs, eager to be the first to get their noses into the food. Tom was nearly knocked flying by Bessie as she brushed one massive shoulder against him, but he somehow managed to keep his balance and started to wade grimly back to Morag. When he finally emerged on to drier ground, he looked down to see that his feet were two clumps of evil-smelling muck.

'What am I supposed to do with these?' he asked.

'They really suit you,' said Morag – but not in her own voice. Tom glanced up in surprise, to see that the girl's pretty face was flickering and melting like a dodgy DVD.

'Morag?' he whispered.

But she was no longer Morag. She had grown another foot in height, her long blonde tresses replaced by a short auburn bob. 'I think you should take them,' said Mum. 'They look really cool.'

Tom looked down again to see that the two blobs of muck had been suddenly, inexplicably, replaced by a pair of bright red Converse sneakers – while the filthy ground beneath them had turned into a stretch of clean blue carpet. He looked up again in dull amazement. Mum was just standing there, smiling at his astonished expression. 'What's the matter? Cat got your tongue?' she asked him. But before he could even think of an answer to that, another figure stepped into view from behind him. It was Dad – Dad dressed in an immaculate black suit with a crisp white shirt and a black silk tie. He was grinning as though everything was fine and dandy.

'Well?' he prompted. 'What do you say? Do you want them or not?'

SEVEN

Tom looked around in stunned silence. He knew exactly where he was. He was in the Schuh store on Market Street in Manchester. He'd been here a few times but never with his Mum and Dad. In fact, he'd called here only last Saturday . . . at least, it seemed to him that it had been last Saturday, though he could no longer be sure – he'd seen the red Converse boots in the window and told himself that he'd treat himself to a pair when he got some birthday money. Now it seemed like his parents were offering to buy them for him, but . . . there were more pressing concerns right now.

'How . . . how did I get *here*?' he croaked.

Mum and Dad stared at him for a moment, as though waiting for a punch-line. Then they exchanged glances and shrugged.

'I blame you,' said Mum, jovially, a tone of voice she *never* used when she was talking to Dad. 'You've been working him too hard. Poor lad's lost his mind.'

Yes, maybe that's it, thought Tom glumly. He'd come back from the seventeenth century with his brains scrambled. How else was he to explain this?

'He hasn't worked *that* hard,' protested Dad, laughing. 'But he has done brilliantly. Four A's!' He looked at Tom. 'And I said if you got three, I'd buy you the boots.'

'A's?' Tom stared at them. 'I've got A's? In what?'

Dad looked confused. 'Er . . . well in English, History, Maths and . . .' He looked at Mum for help.

'Science,' she added. She looked at Tom. 'How could you forget?' she asked him. 'You only got the results yesterday.'

Tom didn't know what to say. He'd never had an A in his life! What in hell was going on here? He noticed a mirror on the wall, a short distance away, and he stumbled over to it to check his reflection, half-expecting to see an unfamiliar face staring back at him. But no, as far as he could see, he looked exactly the same as he had the last time he'd checked.

'Still the best-looking boy around,' said Mum.

'Hey!' Dad warned her and she smiled, bowed her head.

'Still one of the *two* best-looking boys around,' Mum corrected herself and then unbelievably, she stepped closer to Dad and they exchanged a little kiss, right there in front of everyone.

'No way!' cried Tom and they both turned to look at him.

'I think we're embarrassing him,' murmured Dad. Then he looked at Tom. 'You OK, sport? You look a little pale . . .'

'It's . . . warm in here,' murmured Tom.

'Sit down a moment,' Mum advised him. She steered him to a leather bench, pushed him down on to it and then, kneeling in front of him, began to unlace the boots.

'No, I'll leave them on,' he told her. 'If that's OK.'

She smiled. 'I can't say I blame you!' she said. 'God knows how you managed to get these ones so filthy.' She indicated Tom's black school shoes which were encrusted with dried mud. 'Looks like you've been wading through a pigsty,' she said.

Tom stared at her, wondering if she somehow knew what had happened to him. But now she had turned back to Dad. 'Michael, you go and sort out paying for them,' she suggested and handed him Tom's school shoes. 'These can go in the box. And make sure you get a receipt, just in case he changes his mind.' She looked again at Tom. 'You're sure these are the ones you want? You could go for the leather if you prefer; it's only another ten quid . . .'

'No, these are fine,' mumbled Tom. 'Thanks.'

Dad nodded and strolled away.

'You sure you're all right?' asked Mum. 'You seem . . . odd today.'

He glared at her. She looked different from how he remembered. Her hairstyle was pretty much the same, but it looked sharper, glossier. She was wearing a coat he hadn't seen before, a bright red coat, the same colour as her lipstick and nails.

'What are we doing here?' he asked her.

She looked dismayed. 'But you said this was where you wanted to come. If there's somewhere else you'd rather . . .'

'You *know* what I mean! What are we doing back in Manchester? What happened to Edinburgh?' He leaned closer and lowered his voice to a whisper. 'What happened to Hamish?'

She gazed back at him, her expression blank, and he realised that she couldn't have faked it that well. She genuinely didn't have the first idea what he was talking about. Thoughts raced through his mind in a jumble. This wasn't something he had experienced before and nor was it something that was likely to happen to him in the near future. He thought, once again, of Kane in *Timeslyp*, the way he would burst through a series of doors, each of them leading into an alternate reality. Was this what had happened?

Dad came wandering back, a shoebox tucked under his arm. 'Sorted,' he said. He looked from Mum to Tom and back again. 'What now?' he asked.

Mum smiled. 'This is Tom's day. Let's see what he'd like to do.'

Tom could hardly believe it. Mum was asking him what he wanted to do, like it really mattered. He thought for a moment. 'I could eat something,' he ventured. 'I'm quite peckish.'

'Great idea,' said Dad. 'Where do you fancy?'

'*Wagamama's*,' said Tom, without hesitation. It was a kind of test. It was his favourite place to eat but Mum always vetoed it, saying her delicate stomach couldn't tolerate the flavours . . . but not today.

'*Wagamama's* it is,' she agreed and started towards the exit.

Tom got to his feet and followed her. 'But . . . you don't like it there!' he protested. 'You always say the food's too spicy for you.'

Mum shook her head. 'Don't think so,' she said. 'I'm having the chicken katsu curry.'

'And the duck gyoza,' added Dad. 'Don't forget that. With the sticky plum sauce. Mmmm.'

*

Twenty minutes later, Tom was sitting at one of the long wooden tables, watching in amazement as Mum wolfed down a portion of curry as though she'd been eating it all her life. Dad too, seemed to be enjoying his bowl of noodles, as never before, and he'd ordered not one but *three* side dishes. Not bad for a man who previously couldn't seem to make a decision about anything. Tom picked at his own food, staring around the crowded interior of the familiar restaurant and it seemed to him that he was looking at it for the first time.

It was the same but different somehow – bigger, brighter, louder than he remembered it. In the open kitchen, the chefs in their white jackets and red headbands sent up brilliant columns of orange flame from beneath their sizzling woks and shouted instructions at the waiters, who bustled frantically to and fro among the tables in their brightly coloured T-shirts, their electronic order pads held ready for action.

The food in Tom's mouth seemed to explode with flavour – the duck gyoza, rich and succulent parcels dripping with sweet plums; the chicken katsu curry, tender mouthfuls of meat in a thick, glutinous sauce. Dad offered a taste of his noodles, which were springy and crunchy and laced with chilli and fresh ginger. It wasn't usually Tom's favourite dish, but today it tasted like a bowlful of heaven.

I've gone barmy, thought Tom, calmly. There was no other explanation. His accident back in Edinburgh had given him a bash on the head that had sent him into some prolonged hallucination from which he would probably never escape. And what about Morag and her friends, back in the seventeenth century? Was he going to see any more of *them*?

'You know,' said Dad, lowering his chopsticks for a moment. 'We're really proud of you, son.'

Tom nearly laughed out loud at that one. 'Is that right?' he muttered.

'Sure. I mean, you turned it all around, didn't you? Started studying extra hours, made sure your homework was done before you went out. Showed those teachers they were wrong about you.'

'Why are you talking like this?' cried Tom.

Dad held his hands up in mock surrender. 'Yeah, I know, a bit cheesy. But I just wanted to say, well done. Keep on like this, and you'll be headed for university in a couple of years. That is, if you decide it's what you want.'

'Don't pressure the boy,' Mum chided him. 'Just because you went, it doesn't mean Tom wants to follow in your footsteps.'

Tom's jaw dropped. He knew for a fact that Dad had never gone to uni. He'd done a vocational course at an obscure technical college back in Wales. But it was pointless to protest the point. Clearly, in this version of reality, Dad had done rather better for himself. He decided to probe a little more.

'So, Dad . . . your job?'

'What about it?'

'I've never really understood exactly what it is you do.'

Dad laughed. 'Join the club,' he said, but when Tom didn't laugh, he smiled and thought for a moment, as though considering the best way to answer. 'I suppose it's just a case of deciding what a building needs to be and then, thinking about what it *could* be. You have to find the right balance between the two. You know, I always think that architecture is like . . .'

'You're an *architect*?' Tom interrupted him.

Dad laughed. 'Well, yes, you knew that much, didn't you?'

'Er . . . sure,' said Tom. He wanted to add, *you were a painter and decorator last time I checked*. Instead, he turned his attention to Mum. 'And I suppose you're still . . .'

'at the BBC,' she finished. 'Yes, of course; I think I'd have mentioned if there'd been any change.' She gave him a puzzled look. 'I feel like I'm at an interview,' she said. 'You are being a bit odd, Tom, if you don't mind me saying.'

'What happened to the catalogue?' he asked her.

'What catalogue?' She was looking at him blankly, her red painted mouth moving around a mouthful of sticky rice.

The one you used to work for. The words were in his head but he couldn't bring himself to say them, because he knew he'd just get that blank look again, as though he'd started speaking in another language.

He tried to rationalise things in his mind. OK, so he was back and everything had changed for the better. Mum and Dad were together, they both had better jobs, they seemed incredibly happy and he, Tom, had turned into some kind of genius, getting A grades left, right and centre. But . . . it couldn't be as easy as that, could it?

There was a great flash of flame from the open kitchen and Tom turned his head to look. A huge cloud of smoke had momentarily blanketed the chefs from sight and, as it began to clear, he noticed a strange figure standing over by one of the hobs – a thin man wearing a powdered white wig and a fancy gold jacket. He was staring expressionlessly across the rows of tables at Tom. Then he grinned, revealing twin rows of rotten green teeth.

Tom dropped his chopsticks and said something rude. His parents stared at him across the table.

'Steady on, sport!' said Dad. 'There's no need for that kind of language!'

Tom stood up. 'I need to go,' he said. He looked back towards the kitchen. The man seemed to have vanished now but he knew he couldn't just sit here and eat while there was any chance of him returning.

'You've barely touched your food,' observed Mum. 'Are you sure you're not feeling ill?'

'I'm . . . tired,' said Tom. He was already sliding sideways off the bench. Dad started waving frantically to one of the waiters, while he attempted to cram in a last couple of mouthfuls of noodles.

'Hold on a minute,' protested Mum. 'What's the big hurry? Don't you want a pudding?'

'I'll be outside,' he announced and started walking towards the exit.

They drove home in silence. By now, nothing could surprise Tom, so the fact that they were in a brand new BMW X5, rather than the usual five-year-old Vauxhall Astra, had passed without comment. He sat in the back, staring out at the rolling green countryside, while Mum and Dad prattled aimlessly away in the front. Dad was working on a new health centre and Mum was doing a documentary series about the history of theatre, which involved some famous actors. She mentioned their names as though they were old friends of hers. It occurred to Tom that the car didn't seem to be heading towards Withington and, sure enough, a few moments later, he saw a road sign for Wilmslow and realised that this must be yet another change in their circumstances.

Dad pulled the vehicle to the right and stamped on the accelerator as he overtook a slower vehicle. Tom almost laughed hysterically when he saw that it was a black coach being pulled by four horses. Sitting at the reins was an unshaven man wearing a frock coat and a triangular hat. His upraised arm held a leather whip, which he was cracking above the heads of the horses.

'Bloody tractors,' muttered Dad, as he accelerated past.

Tom didn't bother correcting him. He realised now that he was seeing things that his parents couldn't see and it probably wouldn't be a good idea to mention it.

Eventually Dad steered the BMW off the road towards a set of ornate metal gates, which swung magically open to admit them. He drove down a long, gravel drive and pulled the vehicle to a halt outside a three storey, ivy-clad building which looked amazing in the last rays of afternoon sunlight. Tom got out of the car and stood there, looking up at the front of the building, realising for the first time just how successful these new versions of his parents really were.

'How much does a place like this set you back?' he asked.

His dad looked surprised. 'What an odd question,' he said. 'Let's just say I won't be retiring for a few years yet.'

Mum and Dad started up a flight of stone steps and Tom followed them, watched as they unlocked the door and disabled the burglar alarm.

'Home sweet home,' said Tom, and Dad smiled.

'You make it sound like we've been away for ages,' he said.

Tom said nothing. He accompanied them inside and followed them through room after room, each one furnished like something out of a movie. Then Dad announced he was going to his study to finish some work. Mum said she had stuff to do in the kitchen, so Tom said he'd go to his room for a while, even though he had no idea where that might be. He went up a rather grand staircase to the first floor and had a look around. Helpfully, one door had a sign on it that informed him it was TOM'S ROOM.

He pushed it open and stepped inside, stood looking at his new surroundings in awed silence. It was all fantastic, from the top-of-the-range iMac on the black-lacquered writing desk, to the framed posters of his favourite rock bands and the state-of-the-art stereo system complete with iPod dock. It was everything he'd ever wanted and it was all *wrong* somehow; one perfectly assembled, gleaming lie that he knew in his heart could never be his reality.

He felt a sudden tiredness wash over him like a wave, sapping every ounce of energy from his body, so he closed the door and walked over to the bed. He sat down on the immaculate white cotton covers and stared around the room. A sudden scrabbling noise snapped his attention over to one corner, where he saw a sleek grey shape scampering along the base of the wall, and he supposed he should be shocked because the rat was spoiling this perfect vision of how his life could be but, in a weird way, he had almost expected it. The all-powerful weariness was claiming him, pulling him down onto the pillows and he allowed himself to be pulled; he stretched out on the bed and his body seemed to be weightless; it seemed to be floating inches above the mattress. His eyelids came down like shutters and he drifted in a blackness as thick as treacle.

And then he slept.

EIGHT

He woke suddenly, aware of a tickling sensation on his chest. He was lying in bed and a shaft of moonlight, cutting through a window above his head, was illuminating something that was sitting on him, something dark and sleek. His eyes focused and there was a close-up view of a furry, whiskered head and a twitching nose. It took an instant before he realised what he was looking at. Then he gave a yell and thrashed upright and the rat was gone, scampering madly away over the grimy bed covers and on to the bare floorboards.

There was a groan from beside him, the sound of somebody stirring from sleep. Then a voice muttered into his ear with a suddenness that made him start.

'What's the matter with you?' It was Cameron's voice. Tom realised this wasn't his bedroom in Wilmslow. He was back at Missie Grierson's orphanage, in the room under the eaves. The same shaft of moonlight that had shown him the rat now illuminated Cameron's grumpy face. He looked none too pleased to have been woken in such a fashion. 'I swear you're worse than wee Davey!' he complained. 'At least with him it was just snoring!'

'There was a rat,' gasped Tom, his voice ragged with revulsion. 'It was sitting on my chest, looking at me.'

'Is that all?' Cameron rolled his eyes.

'What do you mean is that all? That's disgusting!'

Cameron motioned to him to keep his voice down. 'You'll wake one of the neighbours,' he hissed. 'Like Missie Grierson says, it was probably more scared of you than you were of it.'

'I seriously doubt that,' Tom hissed back. He gazed dismally around the grubby room, taking in the dark beams, the cobwebs and the rough-plastered walls. He realised that he was wearing some kind of rough, textured nightshirt. 'How long was I gone?' he muttered.

Cameron stared at him. 'Asleep, you mean? An hour or so, I suppose.'

'No, I mean . . . I've been *gone,* haven't I? You must have missed me for at least a few hours?'

Cameron was staring at him, mystified. 'I don't know what you're on about,' he said. 'Keep your voice down, you'll wake somebody up and then we'll be for it.'

'Yeah, but . . . I need to get this straight. I was with Morag and the pigs, right? She was showing me how to feed them . . .'

'That was *days* ago,' said Cameron, scornfully. He seemed to think for a moment. 'Five days ago at least.'

'And . . . I've been here all that time?'

'Of course you have. And a right pest you've been, as well.' Cameron gave him a disparaging look. 'You're not ill, are ye? You seem to be . . . rambling.'

'No, it's just . . . I'm mixed up, that's all. You remember I told you yesterday . . . I mean, five days ago . . . that I was really from the . . . the twenty-first century?'

'Oh aye?' Cameron looked as though he really didn't

want to be having this conversation.

'Well, I went back, didn't I? I went back to Manchester.'

'Did ye, now? How long did that take?'

'I don't mean I travelled there. It was . . . like, in my head?'

'Oh, in your head, right. That would take no time at all, would it?'

'Anyway, I was there and everything was sort of different. But in a good way, you know? Like, my Mum and Dad were successful and Dad, he had this BMW X5 . . .'

'A what?'

'It's like a . . . posh carriage with no horses . . .'

Cameron looked even more puzzled. 'Why would he want a thing like that?' he asked. 'It wouldn't *go* anywhere, would it? Unless it was on a hill or something.'

'Well, see, in the future, they have these things called cars? And they drive along, using horsepower. I mean, not a real horse, but this thing called an engine.'

'Like a steam engine? I've seen one of those. It didn't go anywhere though. It was in a woollen mill. Everyone was saying it's the future. It just made a lot of noise, as far as I could see.'

'Yeah, well anyway, I was back and it was mostly great but it didn't feel real, you know . . . it looked real but it didn't *feel* right . . . and there were bits of this world mixed in there too . . . like the guy with green teeth and that rat . . .'

Cameron was starting to look weary. 'Look, Tom, this is all very good but I'm really tired so if it's all the same to you, I think I . . .'

Tom ignored him, 'The question is: is this really

happening? Or am I asleep and dreaming it?'

'I wish *I* was asleep and dreaming it,' complained Cameron, dismally.

'Or maybe this *is* happening and the trip back to Manchester was the dream?' He thought for a moment. 'Just a minute . . .'

'What are you doing?'

Tom had leaned over the side of the bed and was feeling around for his clothes on the floor beside it. His hand brushed against a boot and he picked it up, pulled it close to peer at it. It was a red Converse.

'Yes!' he cried. 'I *did* go back, I really did. But . . . if this came back with me, that means the other reality was as real as real reality. So does that mean that if I go back now, I'll be living in Wilmslow? What do you think?'

Cameron sighed. 'If you want to know the truth, I think you're a bampot.'

'A what?'

'A bampot; an idiot. Now for heaven's sake, let me get some sleep.'

'No, look, I can prove it to you!' Tom put down the boot and scrabbled around until he found his blazer. He reached into the pocket and pulled out his mobile. 'There, look!' he said, holding it into the moonlight. 'I bet you've never seen anything like that before, have you?'

'No,' admitted Cameron. 'What is it?'

'That's a mobile phone. With that I can talk to people all around the world. I just press these buttons, see, and their voice comes out of this bit.'

'Go on then,' said Cameron. 'Show me.'

'Well, I can't. There's no signal here, but if there was . . .'

Cameron let out a sigh. 'Look, Tom, it's late and . . .'

'All right, here's something else for you. Look at this!' He pulled the five pound note from his pocket and held it out for inspection. 'Now, what do you make of that?' he asked.

'Who's that vinegar-faced old biddy?'

'That's the Queen of England!'

'The Queen? I thought they had a King?'

'Not in the future! And see, it says there, Bank of England.' He turned the note over. 'And look here, beside this woman . . .'

'She's even worse-looking than the other one!'

'That's . . .' Tom peered at the signature. 'That's Elizabeth Fry. But never mind who she is, look underneath, look at these dates. 1780 to 1845! There now, what more proof do you need? That's her life from when she was born to when she died.'

Cameron looked at him blankly. 'And?' he muttered.

'It's only 1645!' cried Tom. 'She won't be born for another hundred and thirty five years.'

Cameron stared at him. 'Tom, just because you've got some numbers on a scrap of paper, that doesn't mean . . .'

He broke off as a light came bobbing up the creaking staircase and Tom saw a figure in a long white nightgown carrying a lantern.

'Oh, now you've done it,' said Cameron. 'You've only gone and woken Morag. Now there'll be hell to pay.'

But Morag didn't look angry. She looked frightened.

'You're no' supposed to be up here,' Cameron told her.

If Missie Grierson gets wind of it you'll be in . . .'

'Never mind that,' interrupted Morag. 'You've got to come with me. It's Alison. She's really ill!'

They followed the light of Morag's lantern down the stairs to the second floor. Despite being summer it was chilly, so Tom put on his blazer over his nightshirt and pulled on his new red boots. Cameron donned his jacket too. Morag led them along a damp corridor to a paint-blistered wooden doorway and pushed it open. The room was bare, apart from one simple wooden bed. Alison was lying in it, gazing up at the ceiling and panting as though she'd just been running uphill. As Morag came closer with the lantern, Tom saw that the girl's pale features shone beneath a sheen of sweat.

'When did this start?' he asked nervously.

'She's been feeling tired for a couple of days,' said Morag. 'And she was sick before she went to sleep, tonight. Then she woke me up with that gasping noise and she couldn't seem to speak.'

Tom nodded. He took the lantern from Morag and stepped closer, letting the light of it shine down on to Alison's face. The girl stared up at him, her eyes wide with fright: the pupils shrunken down to tiny pin-pricks. But it wasn't that which drew Tom's attention. It was the red swelling that seemed to be bulging out from under one side of her jaw.

He stepped back with a grunt. He knew exactly what it was; he'd read the descriptions when he'd done the research for the Eyam project and he'd seen the same thing on the waxwork of a child back in Mary King's Close. A buboe: a sure sign of contagion.

She had the plague.

NINE

Tom stood there, looking down at Alison's pale features and he felt a jolt of terror go through him. He told himself not to panic.

'We need to get out of here,' he said quietly. 'She has the plague.'

'No,' said Morag. 'No, she can't have!'

'Trust me; she's got all the signs. We need to isolate her, make sure that nobody else . . .'

He broke off as the light of another lantern came into the room and he saw that it was Missie Grierson, dressed in a grubby ankle-length white nightgown, the unlit pipe still jutting from the corner of her mouth. 'What's all this commotion?' she growled. 'What are you boys doing down here? You know you're not supposed . . .' Her voice trailed off as she caught sight of the frail figure in the bed. 'Merciful heaven,' she said. She moved closer so she could see Alison's face more clearly. 'The good Lord save us,' she whispered.

'Tom thinks it's the plague,' said Morag fearfully. 'Say it isn't so!'

'I wish with all my heart, I could,' said Missie Grierson. 'But has she not the devil's mark at her throat, for all the world to see?'

Morag began to cry and Tom instinctively put an arm

around her shoulders. 'We need to clear out of here,' he told Missie Grierson. 'She could infect all of us.'

'Aye, he's right, shift yourselves!'

They moved to the door and stepped out into the hallway. Missie Grierson followed them and closed the door behind her. 'I'll stay with her,' she said. 'Cameron, get yourself dressed and go and summon Doctor Rae.'

'Oh no!' cried Morag. 'Not him!'

'We have to,' Missie Grierson told her. 'It's a crime to try to conceal the plague; you know that as well as anyone. He'll know what to do for Alison.'

'I know what to do,' said Tom. 'At least . . . I think I do.'

Missie Grierson looked at him doubtfully. 'Ach, what would you know?' she asked him. 'You're just a bairn.'

'I've studied this in school,' he told her. 'You know, the special school, where I learned to read?'

She considered for a moment. 'Speak then,' she said. 'I'm listening.'

'Well, first of all, you need plenty of hot water and some disinfectant . . .'

'Disin-what?'

Tom thought for a moment. 'Soap, then. You must have some kind of soap here, surely?'

'We have lye soap which we launder the clothes with.'

'I guess that's better than nothing. Get the soap and wash Alison from head to toe with it.' He thought for a moment. 'Change her nightie and all the sheets too, everything needs to be as clean as possible.' He pictured the filthy room he had just stepped out of. 'Scrub the floors around the bed, everything,' he suggested.

'The floors?' Missie Grierson looked doubtful. 'What good will that do? I can't help feeling you're talking nonsense.'

'No, no, it's the latest thing,' insisted Tom. 'Trust me on this. I'm not saying it will cure her, but . . . it might stop the infection from spreading. See, plague is caused by flea bites and the soap could help to get rid of them. We also need to think about prevention. There's some natural products that fleas hate, we did it for the Eyam project . . .'

He wracked his brains, trying to remember. His teacher, Miss Roberts, had told the class to search the internet and put together a list of natural ingredients that the people of Eyam could have used to deter the sickness, if only they'd known. But what had been on that list? Something came to him. 'Lavender!' he said. 'That was definitely on there, fleas hate it. And . . . garlic, yes, garlic! Do you have that here yet? Are there any Italian restaurants in Edinburgh?'

'What are you babbling about?' muttered Cameron. 'What's an it-al-yun . . . rest . . .?'

'I mean, a good tavern where they cook posh food! You see, we need to use stuff like garlic because you don't have any antibi–'

He broke off, open-mouthed, because he'd just remembered something. Something important. Something incredible. He put a hand into the pocket of his blazer and pulled out the pack of tablets he'd found five days ago.

'Give her these,' he told Missie Grierson. He looked at the instructions on the pack. 'One now, then two a day: one in the morning, one in the evening, until they're all gone.'

'What are they?' asked Missie Grierson, suspiciously.

He tried to think of a way to explain it that she might accept. 'They're . . . a miracle,' he said. 'It's just good luck that I had them with me but . . . they're . . . er, *Sassenach* pills,' he said. 'Yeah, that's right. They're all the rage in England, everyone's using them.'

Missie Grierson was staring at him. '*Sassenach* pills?' she murmured.

'Yeah, they're the best; trust me.'

'I hope you know what you're doing,' she said.

'I do,' he assured her. 'But just to be sure, we'll get hold of the lavender, and the garlic as well . . . if we can find it.'

Missie Grierson frowned. She was looking at the cardboard pack in her hands as though trying to puzzle something out. Then she glanced at Morag. 'Get dressed, girl,' she said. 'Then go and knock on the door of Mr Stuart, the apothecary.'

'At this time of night?'

'Aye, tell him it's an emergency. Tell him we need some lavender and some . . . garlic, if he has any. Tell him I'll settle his bill next time I see him. And mind you, don't say why you want it.'

'He's bound to ask,' said Morag.

'Let him ask away, but keep yer wee trap shut. News of this will get around fast enough without spilling the information to that old blabbermouth. Now, go on with you.'

'Yes, Missie Grierson.' Morag handed her lantern to Cameron and made as if to re-enter the room but Tom stopped her.

'You can't go in there,' he said.

'But that's where my dress is.'

'You can't wear it, not till it's been washed.'

She looked at him, crestfallen. 'But . . . it's the only dress I have. I can't go out in my nightgown, can I?'

Missie Grierson sighed. 'Go down to the laundry and find something else to wear,' she told her. 'I don't care who it belongs to, put it on for now.' Morag nodded and hurried away. 'Throw that nightgown into a tub with some lye soap, while you're at it.' Missie Grierson shouted after her. She fixed Tom with a look. 'I hope to God you know what you're talking about,' she said, 'for this is going to cost me a pretty penny.'

Cameron looked unsure of himself. 'Am I still to go for Doctor Rae?' he asked.

She considered for a moment and then nodded her head. 'Aye laddie, I'm afraid you'll have to. If it gets out that we've kept quiet about an outbreak, there'll be hell to pay.'

'I don't even know where he lives.'

'Ach, you can't miss it, a big fancy house, away at the furthest end of the High Street. And you've a tongue in your head, haven't ye? You can always ask somebody if you're not sure. Go on with you, time's a wastin'.'

'Yes, Missie Grierson.' Cameron turned away and headed back towards the staircase, leaving Tom and Missie Grierson standing in the hallway.

She shook her head. 'Are you sure all this scrubbing and cleaning is necessary?' she asked him.

Tom nodded.

'Well then, you'd best go down to the kitchen and get

some water on the boil,' she said. 'You'll have to rekindle the fire, think you can manage that?'

'Yes,' said Tom.

He was surprised to find that he knew all about reviving the fire with dry wood, filling the big black cauldron from the outside pump and swinging it over the fire to heat up, though he couldn't remember ever doing such things before. He supposed it must have been a skill he'd picked up in the five or so days that had supposedly elapsed since he'd been feeding the pigs with Morag.

'Anything else?' he asked Missie Grierson.

She nodded grimly. 'Aye,' she said. 'Pray.' Then she opened the door and went back into the bedroom, taking the light of her lantern with her.

Tom was instantly plunged into near darkness and had to grope his way along the hall to the staircase. Then he went down the creaky wooden steps with care, gripping the banister rails as he went. When he finally pushed open the kitchen door, he was momentarily relieved to note that there was some light in there – but then it struck him how out of place this kind of light was in the seventeenth century – the cold, flickering glare of electrical light. He moved forward into the kitchen and felt a shock go through him as he realised where it was coming from: a rectangular box standing on a wooden cupboard over in the far corner of the room. It was a television.

He stumbled closer, shaking his head in disbelief, his incredulity growing as he saw who was currently on screen, filmed in black and white. It was Mum. She had a weird beehive hairdo and was wearing an odd kind of

60's style dress, with puff sleeves, over which she'd tied a white, frilly apron. She was standing in what looked like an American kitchen, stirring ingredients in a glass bowl, humming happily to herself. The camera cut to the door behind her. It opened and Hamish stepped into the house. He was wearing a two-piece suit and carrying a leather briefcase. He was clean-shaven and his formerly receding hair had been trimmed into an immaculate crew cut.

'Honey, I'm home!' he announced and there was a ripple of expectant laughter from an unseen audience. Tom noted that Hamish had somehow acquired a convincing American accent. He put his briefcase down and strode into the kitchen. 'How's my favourite girl?' he asked. She turned and gave him a welcoming hug.

'Why, just fine, honey,' she said and she gave him a chaste peck on the cheek. 'I'm making your favourite apple pie as a welcome home treat.' Hamish turned his head and directed a long-suffering look at the camera.

'Oh, goody,' he said, rolling his eyes, and more laughter swelled from the audience who were clearly in on the joke that Mum was a lousy cook. 'Now, where's Tommy? Is that boy still not back from school?'

'He always walks home with Laura-Sue,' said Mum, fluttering her eyelids. 'I declare, he's getting later and later.'

Just then, the camera cut back to the front door, which opened and a young boy stepped into the hall, to a fresh burst of laughter from the audience. Tom's eyes widened in disbelief. He was looking at a freshly-scrubbed version of himself, wearing a college-style jacket, blue jeans and a baseball cap, which was turned the wrong way on his head.

'Have no fear, Tommy's here,' he announced to nobody in particular. It must have been a catchphrase, because the audience erupted into wild applause as he performed a comical, strutting walk along the hallway into the kitchen. 'Greetings, Ma and Pa,' he said, hooking his thumbs into his leather belt. 'So what's happening?'

'Mom's making her famous apple pie,' said Hamish. He and Tom exchanged glances, then both looked at the camera and rolled their eyes in unison. The audience guffawed.

'You're kind of late, Tommy,' observed Mum, completely unaware that she'd just been mocked. 'Have you been with Laura-Sue all this time?'

'Sure,' said Tom. He threw a knowing look at the camera and waggled his eyebrows. 'She was showing me her autograph collection.'

Mum looked worried. 'Maybe it's time you and your father had a little talk about the birds and the bees,' she said.

'Sure thing,' said Tom. 'OK, Dad.' Pause. 'What did you want to know?'

Now the audience was roaring with laughter. Tom couldn't see that any of it was funny but, more importantly, what did it mean?

The door behind him swung open and Cameron shuffled into the room, holding his lantern. He stopped and stared at Tom.

'What are you doing, standing around in the dark?' he muttered. He set the lantern down on the kitchen table, grabbed his overcoat from a hook on the back of the door and shrugged himself into it.

'I'm not *in* the dark, am I?' said Tom, nodding towards the television, where his American self was now setting his 'parents' straight about a few things, much to the delight of the studio audience. 'Bet you've never seen anything like that before, have you?'

Cameron moved closer, buttoning his coat. 'Of course I have,' he said.

Tom stared at him. 'You've seen a *television*?' he cried.

'I don't know what you call it across the border,' said Cameron. 'Here, we call it a meat safe.' He reached out a hand, gripped the edge of the screen and pulled it forward, to reveal the interior of the box which contained a plate and on it, a dodgy-looking hunk of pork. 'It just keeps the flies off,' he said and he swung the door shut again. The corny sitcom was still playing out on the screen under Cameron's fingertips.

'But . . .' Tom pointed. 'What about that?' he said. 'Can't you see it? That's me . . . or at least, a version of me. And that's my mum and . . .' He broke off, aware that Cameron was staring at him again. 'You . . . you can't see anything different, can you?'

'Tom, as usual, I don't know what you're on about,' said Cameron, but even as he said it, his face was bathed in the cold blue light of the TV screen. He was looking at Tom intently. 'Do you really think you can help Alison?'

Tom swallowed. 'Yes,' he said. 'I think I can.'

'Well, we'll find out soon enough. Now, I need to get a move on; Doctor Rae's house is miles from the Close. What were you doing down here, anyway?'

'Er . . . Missie Grierson asked me to get some water heated up.'

'Well, hadn't you better be getting on with it?' asked Cameron. He strode to the door, threw it open and went down the corridor beyond, his boots clumping on the stone-flagged floor.

Tom stood there, looking at the screen. Now Mom and Hamish were hugging each other, while Tom's other self looked uncomfortable.

'Get a room!' he said and winked at the camera. The audience laughed like they were insane.

Tom had to force himself to make a move. He went to the range and opened the stove door, then took handfuls of kindling from the pile beside it and pushed them onto the glowing cinders. He blew gently and the flames caught hold, began to spread.

When he looked again, the TV was just a meat safe.

TEN

Tom woke alone in the kitchen to the sound of a fist thumping impatiently on the front door. He was slumped in a chair, his back aching and his hands raw. He, Missie Grierson and Morag had worked through the small hours, scrubbing floors, laundering clothes and hanging wreaths of lavender around Alison's bed.

Cameron had arrived back just before dawn, as grumpy as ever. He told them that, when he'd finally got to Doctor Rae's fancy house, he'd found a man waiting by the gateway. He'd told Cameron that the contagion was spreading like wildfire and that the doctor was away dealing with an outbreak in another part of the city. The man had a pen and paper. He took a note of Missie Grierson's address, then told Cameron that he was to go back to his home and hang white cloths in the windows, to warn others that the plague was there. The doctor would call the following day and, until he had visited, on no account was anybody to leave the building.

Of course, this was easier said than done. There were another seven storeys above the orphanage; did the rules apply to them also? In the end, they had climbed up to the various levels, informing people of the outbreak below and had left it up to them to interpret the rules as they saw fit. Missie Grierson had hung a white sheet in one of the grimy casement windows at the front of the building and they all settled down to wait for the doctor's visit. But, as the hours passed and nobody appeared, exhaustion overcame them and they slunk away to their beds, leaving Tom down in the kitchen to keep an eye out for his arrival.

The incessant pounding on the door continued. Tom shrugged off his sleep, got to his feet and staggered across the kitchen into the hall. He hurried to the front door and unlatched it, bracing himself for the sight of Doctor Rae standing there like a demon from hell; instead it was a small, skinny fellow with a pale, rat-like face, who was wearing a close-fitting cloth hat and a white cape draped around his shoulders. He was carrying a leather pouch, from which jutted an array of metal implements. He studied Tom closely, an expression on his unshaven face that suggested there was a bad smell coming from somewhere. He didn't look very well, Tom thought. There were beads of sweat on his forehead and dark bags under his eyes.

'This the house with the plague?' he demanded, as though he hadn't seen the sheet hanging in the window.

'Yes, sir,' said Tom.

'I'm Joshua, assistant to Doctor Rae,' announced the man with evident pride. 'Where's the victim?'

'Upstairs,' said Tom. 'First floor.'

The man nodded, stood to one side and clapped his hands. A second man appeared: a big brawny fellow, dressed like his companion and carrying, in thickly-gloved hands, a metal brazier that was already charged with slumbering hot coals. The two men entered the house, shoving their way roughly past Tom, as if they owned the place. They started up the staircase, their feet clumping hollowly on wood. Only now did The Doctor finally make his appearance, stepping out from the shadows of a doorway, looking absolutely terrifying in his leather cape and mask. He strode up to the door and stood for a moment, gazing down at Tom through grimy red goggles – and the boy could hear the tortured sound of his breathing under the birdlike mask.

'Do I know you?' he growled, his voice a deep, hoarse rasp, muffled by the thick layer of leather.

Tom thought about mentioning that they'd passed each other on a crowded street a week ago, but he thought better of it and simply shook his head. The Doctor lifted his long cane in a leather-gloved hand and tapped Tom's shoulder with it. 'Now, boy, what's your name?' he asked.

'Tom. Tom Afflick. Sir.'

'Well, Tom Afflick, why don't you start by telling me everything that's happened here?' suggested The Doctor.

'Er . . . well, it's this girl called Alison. She's maybe twelve years old? She fell ill last night and now she has a buboe, here.' Tom touched the side of his throat.

The Doctor took a deep breath. 'What know you of buboes?' he asked incredulously.

'I know they're a sign of the plague,' said Tom. 'You usually get them in the neck, the groin or under the armpit. But don't worry; we've already taken precautions to make sure it doesn't spread.'

The Doctor leaned closer. He seemed intrigued. Close up, he smelled of old sweat mixed with the tangy musk of whatever flowers and herbs were packed into the beak of his mask. 'Have you now?' he murmured. 'And what precautions would they be?'

'We've cleaned her up and changed the bedding and her nightdress. We've scrubbed the floor of her room and we've put lavender round the bed . . .'

'Lavender?' The Doctor chuckled throatily, a spine-chilling sound. 'What do you hope to achieve by that?'

'It should help get rid of the fleas,' said Tom. 'You . . . you probably don't know this, but it's flea bites that cause the plague.'

The Doctor laughed again. 'These notions get more fanciful all the time!' he exclaimed. 'I don't know how such wild theories originate. Just last night, an old biddy was trying to convince me it was caused by mischievous elves. Said it was a curse for all the iniquity going on in the Close! Blamed it on one of her neighbours, but it turned out the two women have been feuding for years over the ownership of a piece of land. Elves!' He shook his head 'Now you tell me it's fleas. Who am I to believe, the old woman or you?'

'Me,' Tom advised him. 'I've researched this.'

'Have you indeed? And where did you do that, may I ask?'

'At school.'

'You went to school?'

'Yes, where I'm from *everyone* goes to school.'

'And judging from your accent, you're not from round here.'

'No, sir . . . I'm from Manchester, England.'

'Hmm. How goes the war?'

'The . . . war?'

'I am correct, am I not, in the belief that England is currently embroiled in a civil war?'

'Oh, *that* war! Er . . . yeah, no worries, it's . . . going well.'

The Doctor prodded the roughly-sewn badge on the front of Tom's blazer.

'And what does this signify?' he asked.

'Nothing, sir. This is just my school uniform. And that's the school badge.'

'Hmm. This school . . . they teach you to read and write?'

'Yes, of course.'

There was a long silence. The Doctor seemed to be considering all this information. 'Useful skills,' he said at last. 'And rare enough in one so young.' Then he added, 'Take me to the girl.'

Tom turned and led the way into the house and up the first staircase. The Doctor followed, his heavy boots clumping on wood. When they got to the top of the stairs, they found Missie Grierson waiting on the landing with one arm around Morag's shoulders. The poor girl was so terrified she couldn't even bring herself to look at The Doctor.

'Who have we here?' he croaked.

'I'm Mistress Grierson. I run the orphanage.'

'Then it's you I should see about payment,' said The Doctor.

'Payment?' Missie Grierson stared at him. 'But I thought you were paid by the city council?'

'What, you'd have me risk my life for nothing?' muttered The Doctor. 'It's customary to tip the doctor ten shillings. Of course, if that's a problem, I can take my skills elsewhere . . .'

Missie Grierson shook her head. 'Oh no, sir,' she said. 'I'll . . . find it for you.'

'Good. Have it ready before I leave. And who is this?'

'This is one of my young wards, Morag. As you can see, she's . . . worried about her friend, Alison.'

'She looks frightened to me,' said The Doctor. 'As well she might. The plague is no laughing matter.' He lifted his stick and putting the tip of it under Morag's chin, he lifted her face to look up at him. 'Wheesht, child, don't you worry your pretty little head,' he told her, 'I'm going to take very special care of your friend.'

'She's not going to die, is she?' whimpered Morag.

The Doctor waved a gloved hand. 'I'm not in the habit of making rash promises, but we shall see. There was a time when the onset of the plague meant certain doom but, using the latest techniques, I've achieved some quite remarkable successes. These days, as many as one in ten manages to survive.' He turned and looked at Tom. 'Lead on, boy,' he said.

'Oh, perhaps I should take you,' offered Missie Grierson. 'I've spent the most time with Alison.'

'No need, Madam,' The Doctor assured her. 'You'll be needing to put your hands on that ten shillings. And young Tom here has been expounding his fascinating views about . . . the efficacy of lavender. I'm sure he'll take good care of me.'

'I know it sounds weird to you,' said Tom, 'but you have to . . .'

'Lead on, boy, before the poor girl dies of old age!' snapped The Doctor impatiently, so Tom led him along the landing to the door of Alison's room. When he pushed it open, he saw that The Doctor's two helpers were already in there. The stocky man had opened the small casement window and had placed the glowing brazier in front of it. He was blowing on it to coax fresh heat from the slumbering coals. Joshua had unrolled a leather pouch and was arranging a row of fearsome-looking metal instruments on the floor beside the bed.

As Tom watched, he selected what looked like a poker and thrust the head of it into the midst of the coals. He caught Tom's eye and winked mischievously. Alison looked on, wide-eyed in terror, as well she might. Tom knew from what he had read that the preferred method of dealing with buboes at this time was to cut them open with a razor, drain the pus and insert a red-hot iron into the wound in order to cauterise it. It was not uncommon for patients to die of shock and those few who actually survived the plague would be scarred for life by its drastic treatment.

The Doctor stood beside Tom, staring at the bed. In the small room, he smelled even worse than he had down on the street, like something that had died and been left to rot. He approached the bed and looked at the clumps of lavender hanging from the metal headboard on lengths of twine. He reached out and touched one of them.

'Where did you first hear of this nonsense?' he hissed.

'It's not nonsense!' said Tom, without hesitation. 'It's . . . the latest thing.' He studied Alison and thought she looked a little better than she had the night before. The swelling at her neck seemed to have gone down a bit and she was no longer gasping for breath. 'Honestly, she's looking loads better than she did. I think she's already on the mend.'

The Doctor didn't seem so convinced. He moved closer to the bed. 'Now, my pretty,' he purred, as he leaned over Alison. 'How are we feeling this morning?' He lifted the stick and poked at the red swelling under her jaw, making her flinch. 'Is that sore, my dear?'

'A . . . a little,' gasped Alison, staring up at the hideous beaked mask. 'But nothing like as bad as it was last night. I think the Sassenach pills must be working!' She pointed to the cardboard box of antibiotics on a rough wooden table beside the bed.

'The . . . *Sassenach* pills?' The Doctor reached out and picked up the box. He stared at it for a moment, puzzling over the printed design and the brightly coloured logo. Then his masked head turned to look at Tom again. 'What are these things?' he snarled.

Tom swallowed. 'It's j . . . just some medicine I brought with me from . . . from Manchester.'

'Doesn't look like any medicine I've ever seen. What manner of apothecary despatched these?'

'Oh, just my . . . regular GP! Those pills are made 'specially for the plague.'

'Plague pills?' The Doctor shook his head in disbelief. 'Are you making mock of me? There's no such thing!'

'Not here, but you can get them in England! E . . .

everybody's using them.' As he watched, The Doctor was opening the box and pulling out one of the transparent blister packs. His head tilted to one side as his seventeenth century mindset tried to figure out just exactly what he was looking at.

'You'll see,' Tom assured him, 'she's only had two, so far, but if she finishes the course, she'll be right as rain and the plague will be gone. I guarantee it.' He gestured at the metal implements beside the smoking brazier. 'There's no need for any of that, honestly.'

'I'd say that's for me to decide,' said The Doctor. He slid the blister pack back into its box and threw it almost contemptuously onto the table-top. Then he walked back to the foot of the bed and gestured to his assistants. 'We will continue with the treatment,' he told them. He propped his cane against the end of the bed and held out one hand. Joshua stepped forward and placed an evil-looking scalpel into it. Alison gave a little gasp of terror.

'Don't fret, my dear,' whispered The Doctor. 'A simple cut to release the purulence and then a wee tap with the hot poker and we'll be done . . .'

'No!' said Tom. He stepped forward to bar The Doctor's path. 'No, please, give me another day or so and she'll be as right as rain. I promise.'

The Doctor stared down at him, his eyes glittering dangerously behind the black mask. He seemed to be considering his next course of action. For a moment, Tom feared that he would lift the scalpel and plunge it into his chest.

'You impudent pup!' he hissed. 'You dare to challenge

me, the leading expert in my field?'

'O . . . only because I've worked with an expert too,' Tom assured him. 'In Manchester.'

'Expert? What expert?'

'It was er . . . Doctor . . . Wikepedia,' stammered Tom. 'Yes, he's the talk of the city. Any question you ask him, he knows the answer. He's brilliant. I've worked with him many times. He gave me the pills. He said to me, if I saw anybody with the plague up in Edinburgh, I was to use them.'

There was a long silence, broken only by the sound of a coal cracking in the brazier. Tom looked and saw that deep in the heart of the coals, the head of the poker was glowing bright red. He tried not to think of it making contact with Alison's neck.

The Doctor took a deep breath and then he spoke. 'You are a . . . headstrong boy,' he said. 'One might say, a foolish boy. If you're wrong, this girl's fate will be on your head. However . . . since time is tight and there are other cases waiting . . . ones who might accept the wisdom of an expert in this sickness . . . we shall give you the benefit of the doubt.' He waved a hand at his assistants. 'Out,' he said. 'We go on to the next case.'

The two men looked disappointed but they hurried to obey him. Joshua pulled the poker from the fire and thrust it into a bucket of water. There was a loud hiss as the heat was abruptly quenched. The other man snatched up the smoking brazier and carried it out of the room. Finally, with visible reluctance, Joshua took the scalpel from The Doctor's hand and returned it to its pouch. He followed his companion.

'I'll return tomorrow,' said The Doctor. 'You can be sure of that. And if there's no marked improvement, the girl will be given the prescribed treatment. No arguments. Do you understand?'

Tom nodded, and with that, The Doctor grabbed his cane from the end of the bed and swept out of the room. A moment later, the sound of his heavy boots went thudding down the stairs.

Tom let out a sigh of relief and even Alison managed a pale and weary smile. 'Thank you, Tom,' she murmured. 'I don't know what would have happened if he'd touched me with that poker.'

Tom turned back to face her, realising that the encounter had coaxed a sweat of fear out of him. He lifted an arm and wiped his forehead on the sleeve of his blazer.

'Don't thank me,' he told her. 'Just get better by tomorrow.'

And he went out of the room, closing the door behind him.

Eleven

There was nowhere to go and nothing to do. Because of the white sheet in the window, no customers came to bring laundry and the tenants on the upper floors didn't want to have anything to do with the people living below them – not until the all-clear was given.

Missie Grierson spent much of her time in Alison's room and the children, free from the everyday toil of their trade, moped around the first and second floors like three lost lambs. Tom found himself sitting with Morag in the kitchen. In fact, since his run-in with The Doctor, he couldn't seem to go anywhere without her trailing along after him, looking up at him in some kind of bewildered awe. Clearly she had been very impressed by the way he'd handled himself. He'd sneaked off to the kitchen to try to think about what was happening and what he might do to escape from here but Morag had still found her way to him. He hadn't the heart to tell her to clear off. She was clearly worried and wanting reassurance.

'Do you think Alison's going to be all right?' she asked him fearfully for perhaps the sixth time that day.

He nodded. 'Missie Grierson says she's loads better. She reckons it's her chicken broth that's done the trick, but I know it's the antibiotics . . .' He glanced at her. 'The, er . . . Sassenach pills,' he corrected himself.

'You saved her life,' said Morag, almost as though she thought he might not have realised this. 'She'll always be in your debt.'

Tom shrugged. 'She doesn't owe me anything,' he said. 'It was just lucky I had the pills with me. See, I had this ear infection a while ago but it went away by itself. I'd kind of forgotten I had them.'

'Well it's lucky you did. What's an ear infection?'

'Oh it's just . . . you know, when you get earache.'

'Like when you've been listening to Cameron?' said Morag brightly and Tom grinned.

'Yeah, that would do it,' he agreed.

Morag studied him intently. 'Cameron says you're a bampot,' she said.

'Yeah, I know he does.'

'He says that you keep going on about being from the future.'

'Only because it's true,' insisted Tom.

'But . . . how could you be?'

'I don't really understand it myself.' He thought for a moment. 'Remember when I first met you on the Royal Mile? And I said I'd had a fall?'

She nodded.

'Well, that's what happened to me – only when I began to fall I was in 2012 . . . and when I landed I was here, in 1645. It's like I just . . . fell through time.' He frowned. 'I told Cameron all this but he didn't believe me.'

'I believe you,' said Morag, solemnly.

Tom smiled at her. He reached into his pocket and took out his mobile phone. 'See, I showed him this,' he said, 'I thought it might convince him if I could make it work, but of course I couldn't get a . . .' He broke off in surprise as he saw that the phone's icon was now illuminated. It was only weak: a couple of bars, but it *was* a signal.

He didn't waste any time wondering how such a thing could be possible. He pressed his contacts button and hit his dad's mobile number, noting as he did so that the battery level was already dangerously low. He lifted the device to his ear and listened intently. There was the longest pause and then a ringing tone. It sounded very far away and, Tom thought, *it ought to*. It was travelling hundreds of miles across hundreds of years. He waited, hardly daring to breathe.

'What are you doing?' asked Morag, mystified.

'I'm phoning my dad.'

'But what . . .?'

He waved her to silence. The phone rang again and again and he began to think he was wasting his time. Then–

'Hello?' His dad's voice: faint, distant, but unmistakeably his.

'Dad, it's me! It's Tom!'

'Tom?' A pause. 'Look, mate, you shouldn't really be calling me at work. I'm kind of busy this morning.'

'No, Dad, listen, this is important. Really important. I'm in Edinburgh, right, only not in modern-day Edinburgh. I know it sounds crazy, but it's 1645 and I'm at this orphanage . . .'

Dad laughed. 'That's very funny, Tom, but really, I've got way too much on this morning. You can tell me all about it when I get home, OK?'

'When you . . . get home?' That stopped Tom in his tracks. 'But, Dad, I don't . . . I don't understand.'

Dad answered, talking slowly as if to an idiot. 'When I get home from work, we'll speak then. OK? I'm sure whatever it is can wait a few hours, can't it?'

'But . . . don't you know? About Mum, I mean?'

'What about her?' Dad sounded baffled, a little bit cross.

'She . . . I'm sorry, there's no easy way to say this, but she's . . . well, left you, Dad. She's moved up to Edinburgh with this other guy she met, Hamish. She left you a note and . . .'

'Son, if that's meant to be a joke, it's in very poor taste.'

Tom sat there, open-mouthed, his mind racing. 'But, I . . .'

'And what's all this nonsense about Edinburgh?'

'It's . . . it's where Mum went,' whispered Tom. 'Isn't it?'

There was a long sigh at the other end of the phone. 'Look, I know it hasn't been easy for you,' said Dad, speaking with great care. 'With Mum going so suddenly, it was a great shock for both of us . . . and then all the stress of the funeral and everything, of course it got to us both. But I thought we were over that. I mean, it's been a year now and we both have to go on with our lives . . .'

Dad's voice seemed to fade away to a background murmur. Tom sat there in a state of shock, only vaguely aware of two trickles of moisture running down from the corners of his eyes. He wasn't sure why he was crying. He was pretty sure she wasn't dead, not really, but it was the idea of it that had got to him. Morag was looking at him intently, her mouth open.

'Tom?' Dad's voice: more urgent now. 'Tom, are you still there?'

'Uh . . . yes. Yes, I'm here.' *Wherever 'here' is*, added a voice in his head.

'Look, do you want me to come to school and get you?'

'That er . . . that could be tricky,' croaked Tom. He took a deep breath. 'Tell me . . . tell me about Mum.'

'Tell you about her?'

'About what happened.'

'You know what happened!'

'I just . . . need to hear it. One more time. Please.'

Another long pause. Tom was horribly aware that the battery on his phone was almost drained.

'Well, she . . . Tom, she was driving down to the shops, wasn't she? You know that much.'

'Yeah, but I can't remember *why*.'

'Why? Well . . . she needed to look for a present for Veronica's leaving do, didn't she? And the lorry came out of a side street and I suppose maybe she wasn't concentrating . . .' Dad's voice was ragged, just on the edge of breaking up. 'Look, this is crazy. I don't know why I'm going over it again.'

'Because I need to know!' It came out sounding angrier than Tom had intended, but his parents had never been good at keeping him in the loop. It had come as a complete surprise to him when they'd split up.

Dad sighed. 'They said it was very quick . . . the police . . . they said she wouldn't have known what . . . what hit her . . .' His voice trailed off for a moment and there was the sound of his laboured breathing as he tried to pull himself

· 99 ·

together. 'Tom, do we have to talk about this now? Can't we do it tonight, when I get home from work?'

'Sure. Sure, Dad, I . . . I'm sorry; I just needed to hear the details.'

'But we must have been through it a dozen times.'

'I know. I'm sorry.'

'And you're all right?'

'I'm fine now. I'll . . . I'll see you later. When you . . . when you get home. When *I* get home.'

'OK. Bye, son.'

Dad hung up. Tom sat there, trying to tell himself that this was just another alternative reality; it didn't really mean that his mother was dead. But he couldn't help wondering if – when he got back – if he *ever* got back – would *this* be the world that was waiting for him? What if one of the crazy things he'd been shown could actually come true? What then?

TWELVE

He realised that Morag was still looking up at him intently.

'Are you all right, Tom?' she whispered. 'I heard a wee voice coming from that thing. Like an imp in a bottle.'

Tom nodded. He sniffed, wiped his eyes on his sleeve. Then a thought occurred to him and he hit the button on the phone that would display the few photographs he had stored on there. He found the only one he had of Mum. She was standing in the kitchen at home, looking awkward because she never liked having her picture taken, but Tom thought it was a good one of her; she looked young and pretty, her dark hair brushed and shining. He held out the phone to show the image to Morag.

'Oh, what a lovely miniature,' she said.

'That's my mum,' said Tom. 'And it's not a painting, it's a photograph.'

'She looks very grand,' said Morag. 'What are those things behind her?'

'Hmm?' Tom looked. 'Oh, that's just a kettle and a toaster. You make tea or coffee with this thing and you toast bread in that. You just press a button and when it's ready, it pops up.'

'I see,' said Morag. 'But where are the flames?'

'There aren't any. It just . . . gets hot. You heat the bread till it's brown and you put butter on it and maybe some

Nutella or something…' He looked at her blank expression. She clearly didn't have a clue what he was talking about. 'Anyway,' he said, 'I just wanted to show you my mum.'

'It's very lifelike,' said Morag. 'You can't even see the brushstrokes.'

'No, that's because there aren't any. I took this myself. Here, look. I'll take one of you.' He lifted the camera and framed Morag in the shot. 'Smile,' he said, but she just opened her mouth to ask something. He snapped the picture anyway. Then he turned the camera back to show her. There she was, sitting in her chair, her mouth open, a puzzled expression on her face.

When she saw the photograph, Morag let out a gasp of surprise. 'How did you *do* that?' she cried.

'It's no big deal; everybody can do it where I come from. You just need a mobile phone.'

'But that's incredible!' she cried. 'Tom, I think you really are from the future!'

Just at that moment the door opened and Cameron shambled into the room, looking bored.

'Cameron!' cried Morag. 'You must come and look at this.'

He glanced at the device in Tom's hand. 'I've already seen it,' he said, his voice toneless. 'That's the machine that Tom uses to talk to people all over the world. Only it doesn't work.'

'It does actually,' Tom assured him. 'I just spoke to my dad, in Manchester.'

'Did you really? That's nice. And what did he have to say for himself?'

'He told Tom something about his mother,' said Morag. 'I could hear a wee voice speaking but I couldn't make out the words. What was it he said to you, Tom? About your mother. The thing that made you cry?'

'He told me she was dead. Only . . . I'm pretty sure she isn't, not really.'

'Oh, right, that's as clear as mud.' Cameron nodded wearily, an expression of complete boredom on his face. 'Is there anything to eat in here? I'm starving!'

'But you haven't seen me on the picture box,' insisted Morag. 'Tom just used it to paint a wee picture of me and it only took him a moment to do it.'

'You're as barmy as he is,' muttered Cameron.

'Come and look if you don't believe me!' cried Morag.

Cameron sighed and began to plod over to them but, in that same instant, the battery finally gave out and the screen went black.

He peered at it for a moment and then said, 'It's not the most flattering picture I've ever seen.'

'That's not it!' cried Morag. 'It's gone. Tom, bring it back again!'

'I can't,' he said mournfully. 'The battery's gone.'

'Gone?' She looked around the room. 'Gone where?'

'You don't understand. It needs recharging. I don't have a charger with me and, even if I did, I'd need somewhere to plug it in.'

'See,' said Cameron. 'There's always something that doesn't quite work, isn't there? Show her the piece of paper with the old woman's face on it. Maybe that'll convince her.'

Tom scowled. He slipped the useless phone back into

his pocket. 'You're always too slow,' he snarled. 'You miss everything.'

'Oh, excuse me!' sneered Cameron. 'I may be slow, but at least I'm not a bampot. At least I know what's real and what isn't.'

'Tom's *not* a bampot!' cried Morag. 'He's telling the truth about being from the future. I've seen proof.'

'You'd believe anything he tells you,' snapped Cameron. 'Trotting around behind him like a wee lapdog; you're ridiculous.' He slipped into a parody of Morag's high-pitched voice. 'Ooh, Tom, Tom, you're so brave talking to Doctor Rae like that! You're my hero!' He shook his head. 'Can't you see he's just reeling you in with his fancy lies.'

Suddenly, Tom couldn't help himself. He was up out of his chair and striding towards Cameron. 'You take that back!' he shouted.

'I will not. It's the truth. You're mad and you're turning her the same way.'

'Take it back!' Tom reached out a hand and pushed Cameron hard in the chest. 'Or else . . .'

'Or else what?' sneered Cameron. He bunched his hands into fists. 'What are you going to do about it, bampot?'

Something in Tom snapped. He threw a wild punch that caught Cameron on the chin, flinging him backwards across the kitchen and slamming him up against a wall. Cameron looked dazed for a moment. He wiped his mouth on the back of one hand and grinned maliciously.

'Right then,' he said. He came back at Tom, fists swinging. Tom managed to duck the first blow but, as he straightened up the next one thudded into his stomach, doubling him over. He managed to swing an arm up at Cameron, pushing him away, and the two of them grappled for a moment, flailing wildly around the kitchen like they were dancing with each other.

'Stop it!' cried Morag. 'Stop it at once; somebody is going to get hurt!'

'That's the idea,' snarled Cameron and then yelped as a punch from Tom caught him on the ear. He retaliated, flinging more punches in return. His left hook missed completely but the right one went full into Tom's face and connected with his nose. Fireworks seemed to go off inside Tom's head, a riot of colourful explosions – and for an instant he was a little kid again – he was with his mum and dad at a firework display; they were pointing up at the rockets exploding in the sky and saying, 'Oooooh' and 'Aaaaah!' and he was laughing wildly because he was so excited and also a little scared by the noise.

But that was only for an instant, because then a black hood seemed to drop over his head and shoulders and he was falling in slow motion, a horrible sick feeling lurching in his stomach. The hood came off and now he was falling amidst a confusion of dust and broken floorboards and lumps of stone. He looked up and saw a grey, flickering Morag gazing down at him through a large ragged hole in the floor above. There was concern in her eyes, but suddenly she wasn't Morag any more; she was Mum, standing in the kitchen, smiling and telling him to take the picture quickly, before she changed her mind; she hated having her photograph taken. And he was just going to say 'Smile' when something hard slammed against his back, driving the breath out of him and he lay there, gasping, as everything around him shifted in and out of focus . . .

And he was back in the kitchen of the orphanage. Morag was kneeling beside him, crying her eyes out and telling Cameron that he'd killed Tom. Cameron stood beside her, shaking his head, saying that he'd only given the lad a wee tap and didn't it serve him right for starting something he couldn't finish? Then the door opened and Missie Grierson strode into the room.

She stood there, looking down at them, her hands on her plump hips. 'What in the name of reason is going on here?' she shouted.

'Cameron's trying to kill Tom!' shrieked Morag.

'Ach! He struck the first blow,' argued Cameron. 'I'm sick of him walking round saying mad things all the time. It serves him right.'

Missie Grierson took the clay pipe from her mouth and let out a great cloud of smoke. 'Haven't we enough trouble to contend with, without you bairns going at each other like wild animals?' she cried. She glared at Cameron. 'You,' she said. 'The pigs still need their food, even if we have precious little for ourselves. Get out there and feed them.'

'Oh, but Missie Grierson, Tom–'

'Out, I say! Morag, you go with him.'

'Do I have to?' complained Morag.

'Aye. Don't vex me, girl. I've had enough trouble for one day and I'm likely to take a switch to your backside. Now, go on, the pair of you.' Cameron walked over and collected the scrap bucket. He headed grumpily towards the back door. Morag trudged after him.

Missie Grierson stood there, looking down at Tom. 'Well, don't just lie there, boy, get yourself upright.' She fished in a pocket and found a grubby kerchief, which she pressed into his hand as he struggled to his feet. 'Clean yourself up,' she said. She indicated that he should take a seat and then settled into the one beside him. She watched as Tom dabbed at his bloody nose. 'You all right now?' she asked him.

He nodded.

'What was the fight about?'

'Oh, it was just something that Cameron said about me. He keeps saying that I'm not right in the head. But he doesn't understand. I'm just *different*.'

Missie Grierson nodded. 'I'll tell you what I know,' she said. 'There's a young girl in the room above who's just made the most miraculous recovery in history and it's all due to you and your magic pills.' She took a couple more puffs on her pipe and looked at him intently. 'So yes, I think you are different. I also think it's time you told me the truth, Tom. Who are you? And where did you come from?'

THIRTEEN

Tom lay in an improvised bed on the kitchen floor, unable to sleep. Beside him, Cameron was snoring gently, his back turned. Tom had tried apologising to him earlier and had even offered to shake the boy's hand, but Cameron would have none of it and he hadn't spoken a word to Tom since the fight.

Because of the quarantine situation, the boys couldn't go up to their usual room under the eaves of the building and this was the only solution that Missie Grierson had been able to come up with: a jumble of bedding laid out on the hard slabs of the kitchen floor, a Spartan arrangement that made the meagre bed in the roof-space seem like paradise by comparison. Whichever way Tom tried to stretch himself out, he could feel the chill touch of the stone slabs pressing through the woollen blankets beneath him and he was left to lie there, thinking about what had happened earlier.

He'd told Missie Grierson everything, leaving nothing out. To be fair to her, she'd listened patiently to what he had to say, but the look on her face suggested that she was beginning to think Cameron's opinion of Tom was spot on. A bampot. Tom couldn't blame her. He wouldn't have believed it if somebody else had fed him a similar story. It was absolutely mental. There was no other way of describing it.

The problem was, he had no proof now of where he'd come from. The phone had packed up completely and when he'd shown her the five pound note, she'd just looked baffled. When Tom finally asked her if she believed him she could only shrug her massive shoulders and say that she'd have to think about it, long and hard, before she could offer him an answer.

Now what else was there for him to do but try to get on with the crazy, scrambled life that had been handed to him and hope that, one day, he'd somehow get back to where he'd come from?

A scrabbling sound made him look up and, in the rays of moonlight filtering in through the room's one window, he saw a rat creeping along the wall, the same rat he had seen before, of that he was pretty sure, though he couldn't for the life of him think why. Didn't all rats look pretty much the same? This one was moving forward in a straight line, as though it knew exactly where it was going but, when it was about halfway across the room it unexpectedly stopped and turned to look at Tom. Tom felt a chill go through him. It was almost as though the rat knew him and had stopped to say hello. It raised itself up on its hind legs and stayed where it was for the moment, peering at him, its nose twitching agitatedly.

'Shoo!' hissed Tom, not wanting to wake up Cameron, who was in a bad enough mood already. 'Go away!'

The rat tilted its head to one side, as though trying to puzzle out what Tom had said. Then it dropped back onto all fours and began to approach the bed. A sense of total dread settled over Tom. He lay there, his skin crawling, his heart thudding in his chest, hardly daring to breathe as the rat came steadily closer. It reached the foot of the bedding and hesitated, sniffing at the blankets, as though trying to figure something out. Then it came on again. It crept up onto the grimy covers and moved closer, closer, staring at Tom intently all the while. He lay there mesmerised, aware of beads of sweat popping on his brow and running down his face. He wanted to scream out loud but somehow couldn't make a sound.

And then, almost before he knew it, the rat was on his chest; it was staring at him as though it knew something and wanted Tom to know about it too. And then, most incredible of all, it reared onto its back legs again and spoke in a tiny, whispering voice.

'He's not what he seems,' said the rat and, with that, it whipped around, scampered back along Tom's prostrate form and onto the floor. It went straight back to the wall and resumed its former course, as though it had dismissed Tom completely. He saw the dark shape of it scuttling along until it passed out of sight behind some wooden barrels.

Only then did he remember to breathe.

'No way,' he murmured. Now he knew he really had lost it. Never mind going back in time to 1645, never mind the unplanned visits to various family units that could never be; now he'd been spoken to by a rat! And what had it said to him? *He's not what he seems.* What was that supposed to mean?

Beside him, Cameron murmured something in his sleep and then gave a really creepy-sounding laugh.

'Great,' muttered Tom. He snuggled deeper into the so-called bed and pulled the grotty covers up over his head. He tried to put his mind in the drawer labelled 'sleep' but he had a hard time of it and it was only in the early hours of the morning that he finally located a small gap at the back of the drawer and dropped through it like a coin, into a deep, dreamless darkness.

He woke alone, with the early morning sunlight streaming onto his face and the sound of a fist banging repeatedly on the front door. He lay for a moment, staring blearily around. There was no sign of Cameron. Why hadn't he woken Tom when he got up? Still in a bad mood, most probably, wanting to make him look like a layabout.

Now Tom could hear the sound of voices out in the hall, Cameron's voice, he thought, followed by a hoarse, muffled rasp that could only have belonged to one person. The talking seemed to go on for quite a while before it was replaced by the thudding of heavy boots going up the stairs.

The sound galvanised Tom into movement. He clambered out of bed and hurriedly dressed himself, longing, not for the first time, for his real home, where he would have showered himself fully awake with soap and hot water. He went out into the hallway to find the front door left ajar, and now he could hear voices coming from up on the first floor. He hurried up the stairs and found Missie Grierson, Morag and Cameron standing outside Alison's room.

'What's happening?' he asked them. 'Why didn't somebody wake me?'

'I thought you could use the sleep,' Missie Grierson told him. 'Doctor Rae's in with Alison now.'

Tom realised that he was probably supposed to wait out here too, but somehow couldn't bring himself to do it. He walked past the others and, pushing open the door of the room, went inside. Alison was sitting up in bed, looking perfectly relaxed, while The Doctor bent over her like a huge, black bat, checking her neck for signs of infection. By the window, the man had the hot brazier ready and he also had the metal implements slung across his shoulders, but there was no sign of Joshua this morning. The Doctor turned his masked head and stared at Tom as he entered the room.

'Ah, the magician returns,' said his muffled voice. He picked up the packet of pills from the bedside table and strolled towards Tom, tapping the cardboard box rhythmically against his leg. 'There's quite a transformation here. The girl appears completely cured. No sign of that buboe she had yesterday. No sign whatsoever.'

Tom smiled proudly. 'That's great,' he said. 'I told you those pills would do the trick.'

The masked head nodded. 'So you did, boy, so you did. But I find myself wondering how was this miracle cure effected?'

'Er . . . I told you. The pills.'

'And what, pray, are the ingredients?'

Tom shrugged. 'How would I know?' he muttered. 'They're just pills that you get from the doctor. Medicine. I don't know what's *in* them.'

'But you must have been there when your Doctor . . .

forgive me, I forget his name. Something Latin, wasn't it?'

'Doctor Wikepedia.'

'Yes . . . he must have shown you the ingredients when he made them.'

'Ah, no, it's not like that, not where I come from. You just hand in your prescription and, ten minutes later, somebody comes out with the pills. And they don't make them there, obviously; they'll be made in a factory or something. I mean they must make millions of them . . .'

'Millions? You can get millions of these pills?'

'Er . . . I didn't say I could *get* them, I'm just saying they make a lot.'

The Doctor gestured at Alison, still sitting up in bed and smiling at Tom.

'How do you feel, my dear?' he asked her.

'Much better,' said Alison. 'A little weak, maybe, but nothing more.'

'Hmm.' The Doctor turned back to look at Tom. 'Of course, there are some who would say that what you have done here borders on witchcraft,' he hissed.

Tom shook his head. 'Oh no, it's nothing like that, it's, er . . . science.'

'Well, as a scientific man myself, I am delighted to hear that. Only . . .'

'Only what?' asked Tom.

'I spoke to your young friend Cameron on the way in this morning. He told me a few interesting things about you.'

'Did he?' asked Tom, doubtfully. 'Oh, well, I think he's just in a bad mood with me, because . . .'

'He told me that you're given to strange hallucinations.'

'Really? Umm . . .'

'He says that you arrived here with some ridiculous notion about being from another time. That you fell through it.'

'Hah. As if!'

'He says that you claim to have an imp in a bottle which allows you to speak to people all over the world . . .'

'Oh. When you put it like that, it does sound kind of dodgy,' admitted Tom. 'But there's a perfectly logical . . .'

'So here's what I suggest. I'll take the rest of these Sassenach pills . . . and you'll come along with me.'

'With you? What do you . . .?'

'Actually, it's a very propitious time. My right-hand man, Joshua, has taken a bad dose of the contagion himself and I find myself in urgent need of an assistant. I have decided to confer that honour upon you.'

Tom stood there, hoping that The Doctor didn't mean what Tom thought he meant.

'You're saying . . . you want me to do Joshua's job? Heating up the pokers and all that? I . . . I can't do that. I've got . . . stuff to do here.'

The Doctor placed a gloved hand on Tom's shoulder with a grip so tight it made him wince.

'Oh, but I insist,' he said. 'I think, with the right training, you'll make an excellent stickman.' He spun Tom around and grabbed him by his collar, then started marching him towards the door. 'We'll be on our way, shall we?' he growled. He beckoned with his cane for the brazier man to follow him.

'No! No, wait!' Tom was propelled out of the room onto the landing, where he saw his three companions waiting for him. Missie Grierson and Morag had looks of horror on their faces, whereas Cameron could barely conceal his glee. 'Please! No! I . . . I can't help you. Missie Grierson, *tell* him!' he pleaded.

'Doctor Rae!' Missie Grierson took a step forward to bar The Doctor's path. 'I must protest! Young Tom is my ward. I'm the one who has been charged with his upkeep. I'll no' stand for you taking him away.'

The Doctor paused to look at her, his eyes glittering spitefully behind the mask. 'You'll no' stand for it?' he echoed mockingly. 'My dear woman, you will do exactly as you're told. You'll need my permission to remove the white cloth from your window and, unless the boy comes with me, I'll see to it that it stays there until hell freezes over.' Missie Grierson took a step back as though she had been slapped in the face.

'You . . . you can't do that!' she protested.

'Try me,' suggested The Doctor. 'I think you'll find, Madam, that in the current crisis, I have more powers than you might think. And another thing . . .'

'Yes?'

'There's the little matter of ten shillings that you forgot to give me yesterday.'

'But you didn't treat Alison, so I thought . . .'

'It's ten shillings per visit,' The Doctor assured her. 'So that's nearly two merks you owe me – a sum I'm prepared to overlook if the boy comes with me.'

Missie Grierson stared at him defiantly for a moment,

but then lowered her head in defeat.

'No!' cried Morag. 'No, Missie Grierson, you can't let them take him!'

'I have to, child,' muttered Missie Grierson. 'If we can't do laundry, we can't survive. None of us. And twenty shillings is more than I have in the world.' She looked at Tom. 'I'm sorry, lad,' she said.

Then Tom was being propelled onwards towards the staircase. The Doctor's assistant followed, thrusting the glowing hot brazier towards Missie Grierson to make her step back.

'Goodbye, bampot!' snickered Cameron and Tom felt an overwhelming desire to run back and punch him, but he was helpless in The Doctor's powerful grip. He was pushed and prodded down the staircase and out of the open front door, into the crowded street. 'Meet me later,' The Doctor told the brazier man, 'at the Four Talons.'

'Aye, sir!' said the man and he disappeared into the jostling crowd.

'This way, boy,' said The Doctor and he pushed Tom along in front of him, parting the crowds ahead with an imperious sweep of his cane. Tom struggled to break free but the hand that held him had fingers that felt like steel cables and he could do nothing but stumble forward. After a few moments, he heard a voice calling his name. He looked back and saw that Morag was running after him.

'Tom!' she cried. 'Tom! Don't go, please!'

'Get away, you little fool!' The Doctor lashed out with the cane and she fell back a couple of steps, shielding her face with her arms.

'Morag, go back!' Tom shouted to her. 'It's no use! I have to go with him.'

'I won't forget you,' she called after him. 'Not as long as I live, I promise.'

He managed to wave to her before The Doctor thrust him onwards.

They emerged from the Close onto the broader sweep of the High Street where a horse and carriage was waiting. The Doctor signalled to the driver and the man threw open the door. The Doctor lifted Tom clear of the cobbles and all but flung him head-first into the carriage, then climbed in behind him. 'Coachman, ride on!' he bellowed.

There was the sound of a whip cracking on the air and the coach began to rattle forward. Tom struggled around onto his knees and scrambled towards the open window. He leaned out and saw Morag standing at the top of the Close, a forlorn look on her face. She lifted a hand and waved to him. He waved back and then the horses plunged onwards and she was lost to sight.

A gloved hand grabbed his collar and jerked him back into the coach, then pushed him onto a seat. He found himself sitting opposite the cloaked and hooded figure of The Doctor.

There was a long silence as they sat, looking at each other. Then, lifting his arms, The Doctor reached up and removed his hood.

Tom stared. He sat there, mouth open, trying to find words and when they finally did come, they were the only ones that seemed appropriate to the situation.

'Bloody hell,' he said.

FOURTEEN

He was looking at Hamish – or at least, somebody very like him. Oh, the face was somewhat leaner and there was a shock of thick, oily black hair hanging to his shoulders, but he had the same brutish features, hooded grey eyes and wide, splayed nose that looked as though it had been broken at some point back in the past, most likely by a well-placed fist. The mouth was the same too: a thin-lipped slit which fronted a collection of irregular yellow teeth. The mouth currently held a disapproving scowl. Clearly, The Doctor did not approve of the language that Tom had just used.

'Watch your mouth, boy,' he growled. 'Or is that the kind of language they teach you south of the border?' In the juddering, swaying confines of the carriage, his body odour was simply appalling. Tom was almost afraid to breathe. 'What are you staring at?' snapped The Doctor.

'Sorry,' muttered Tom. 'It's just . . . you look like my Mum's bloke.'

'Your Mum's *what*?'

'Her . . . boyfriend.' Tom hated even saying the word. Why did The Doctor look like Hamish? What did it mean? He made a valiant attempt to change the subject. 'Where are we going?' he asked.

'To my house,' said The Doctor, matter-of-factly.

'Where I can keep a close eye on you.' He reached into his cloak and pulled out the packet of antibiotics. He opened it and withdrew what remained of the blister pack, then did a slow count of the contents. 'Ten pills,' he murmured.

'You shouldn't have taken those,' Tom told him. 'Seriously. Alison was supposed to finish the course. She could get ill again.'

'Nonsense,' said The Doctor. 'She was completely cured. I examined her neck. The buboe had gone, as though it never existed.' He stared at Tom. 'Do you have any idea how important these things are?' he whispered. 'They are worth a fortune!' He thought for a moment. 'How many did the girl take?'

Tom considered. 'Six,' he said.

'So there's enough here to cure two more cases?'

Tom shrugged his shoulders. 'Like I said, you're supposed to take the whole course, really. That's what the doctor told me, anyway.'

'Well, we can definitely cure at least one person,' said The Doctor. 'And the first thing we'll do when we get home is write to this Doctor Wikipedia and ask him for more pills. I don't suppose you've any idea what goes into them?'

Tom shook his head. 'I haven't a clue,' he said.

'So how did you get hold of them?'

'Well, I saw the doctor and he wrote me a prescription and I took it to a chemist . . .'

'A chemist? Is that like an apothecary?'

'I . . . I think so.'

'And the doctor tells the apothecary what ingredients to put in the pills?'

'Er . . . no . . . not really. The pills are already made. The chemist just has to get them off the shelf. It's . . . easy, really.'

'So, there's a multitude of these things, sitting on a shelf somewhere?' said The Doctor, excitedly.

'Well, yes, but . . .'

'So it shouldn't take long to get our hands on a large quantity of them!'

Tom decided it would be easier for the moment to just play along.

'I . . . guess,' he said. 'Sure, why not?'

'When you tell Doctor Wikipedia about the situation here . . . how desperate the plight of the Edinburgh people is. . . I'm sure he'll agree to send us what we need. It'll take a couple of weeks to get hold of them, of course . . . but once I have them . . . I'll be the most powerful man in the city.' He leaned back in his seat and smiled. 'For the time being, we'll just need to pick the next case very carefully. Somebody who will be suitably grateful to have the exclusive rights to the only *Sassenach* pills in Edinburgh. Somebody of means.' He rubbed a thumb and forefinger together, a gesture that hadn't changed over the centuries.

'You mean, you'll ask them to pay?' asked Tom. 'That's not fair.'

'Whoever said life is fair, boy? 'Who pays the piper, calls the tune.' You'd do well to remember that. And it's hardly my fault that we only have ten pills left.' He looked puzzled. 'You said the girl took six tablets – but there must have been eight in the first pack to begin with. Who had the other two?'

'I did,' muttered Tom.

'You . . . you had the plague?'

'No, I had a sore ear. It got better.'

The Doctor looked at him in disbelief. 'Doctor Wikipedia gave you the pills because you had a sore ear?'

'Yes, well that's how it is where I come from. Whatever's wrong with you, you go to see a doctor and he fixes you up, gives you whatever you need.'

The Doctor scowled. 'I've never been south of the border,' he said, 'but I know people who have. None of them seemed to have a good word for what they found there.'

'That must be because they never came to Manchester,' said Tom. 'It's different there.' The coach bucked over something in the road with a force that nearly threw Tom out of his seat and he had to grab the door of the coach to steady himself. He took the opportunity to slide his arm out of the carriage window and grasp the handle. 'Look, I'm not being funny,' he said, 'but when can I go back to the orphanage? They need me there.'

The Doctor seemed amused by this notion. 'Why would you want to go back to that hell-hole?' he cried. 'I'm offering you respectable employment, a decent roof over your head, a square meal in your belly. I dare say you don't get any of that at Missie Grierson's.'

'Maybe not, but, working for you, it's only a matter of time until I go down with the plague like Joshua.'

'That *was* unfortunate,' admitted The Doctor. 'Joshua was one of my longest serving assistants. Must have been with me for near on three months. I'm going to miss him.' He gave Tom a flat stare. 'Forget about the orphanage,' he said. 'You work for me, now. You'll no' be going back.'

Tom frowned. 'How much do I get paid?' he asked.

'Paid?' The Doctor sniggered. 'Well, we'll have to see about that. If you can get me more of those pills, I might be inclined to cut you in for a small percentage but, don't forget, I'll be feeding you and providing you with a place to live. That's worth more than any pay.'

He began to replace the pills into the pocket of his cape and Tom made his move. He turned the handle of the door, then slid along the seat with the intention of throwing himself out onto the road – but he had reckoned without The Doctor's quick reactions. Before he could even raise himself up, a fist connected with the side of his head, flinging him back against the seat rest, his head spinning. As he turned to look at The Doctor, a gauntleted hand slapped him across the face while another yanked the door shut again. Then The Doctor leaned forward, so close that Tom almost retched from the stink of his breath.

'Let's get something straight, boy!' he roared. 'I am your Master now. When I say jump, your only question is: 'How high?' Do you understand?'

Tom nodded, his eyes blurring with tears.

'And, as to your earlier question, you'll no' receive one farthing in payment. Your reward will be the honour of serving me and working to make Edinburgh's streets free from contagion. Do I make myself clear?'

'Yes,' gasped Tom.

'Yes, what?'

'Yes, *Sir*!'

'That's better.' The Doctor eased himself back in his seat

and smiled a twisted smile. 'You know, most lads would be grateful for such an opportunity,' he observed. 'Clearly, ingratitude is something that is instilled in you Sassenachs from birth.'

The coach began to slow and Tom wondered if they had reached their destination – but The Doctor took the opportunity to put his leather hood back over his head, as though expecting something to happen. After a few moments, the coach slowed to a halt alongside another coach facing in the other direction.

Through the open window, Tom caught sight of a shadowy figure sitting in the gloom of the coach's interior and, as he watched, a gloved hand emerged from within and handed The Doctor a single roll of paper. The Doctor took it, nodded briefly to his opposite number and then shouted to the coachman to giddy up. The coach clattered forward again, gathering speed. After a few moments, The Doctor removed the hood. He untied the ribbon from around the paper and peered at its contents with considerable interest. As far as Tom could make out, it was some kind of handwritten list.

'Who was that?' he asked.

The Doctor glared at him. 'Keep your nose out of what doesn't concern you,' he snapped. 'Or is it another slap you're wanting?' He thrust the list at Tom. 'Here, you told me before that you could read,' he said. 'Tell me what's written there.'

Tom looked at him. 'Can't *you* read it?' he asked.

'My eyesight's poor,' said The Doctor. 'Joshua used to perform such duties for me.'

Tom frowned but obediently started to read aloud, as best he could. The list was written in an ornate hand and had some very odd spellings, which made it hard to decipher. It was just a list of names and addresses, none of which meant anything to Tom, but The Doctor listened intently, as though considering each one in turn. Then Tom got to a name that *did* seem to ring a bell, Lord Kelvin.

The Doctor let out a grunt of satisfaction and Tom found himself wondering where he had heard the name before. He continued reading and, when he had finished, The Doctor took the list from him and pushed it into the pocket of his cape. 'Lord Kelvin,' he muttered. 'Well, well, well . . .'

Tom's mind was racing. What had the brief meeting been about? There had been something very secretive about it: the other man keeping himself out of sight; The Doctor taking great pains to ensure that he was masked. And who were the people on that list? It was clear that something was going on and, whatever it was, it was dodgy; of that Tom was sure.

The Doctor didn't speak again for the duration of the journey and, some twenty minutes or so later, the coach came once again to a grinding, juddering halt. The Doctor pushed open the door and climbed out. Then he turned back, threw up a hand and grabbed Tom's lapel, pulling him out of the carriage and down onto the cobbled street. Tom turned to see that they were standing in front of a soot-blackened house, with dirty windows and rotting frames.

'Home, sweet home,' said The Doctor. He flicked a coin

up to the coachman and, grabbing Tom by the scruff of the neck, frogmarched him up the steps and in through the paint-blistered door.

They found themselves in a grimy, windowless hallway, lit by the dull glow of oil lamps. To one side, a staircase led upwards and, beside it, there was a large wooden enclosure, filled with straw: the kind of place where you might keep an animal. Tom immediately knew something was wrong. Cameron had described Doctor Rae's house as a fine, two storey building of grey stone set in its own grounds – and though this place was bigger and more imposing than the tenements of Mary King's Close, still it looked grim and forlorn, badly in need of cleaning.

The Doctor let go of Tom long enough to pull off his heavy leather cloak and hang it on a hook on the wall. He hung the hood beside it. Then he turned back as a door opened and an old woman came out into the hallway to meet them. She was ancient and infirm, her back stooped, her face an assortment of lines and wrinkles, out of which one tar-black eye stared at Tom intently.

'Who's this?' she croaked, in a voice as worn out as her body.

'Mother, meet my new assistant, Tom,' said The Doctor. 'He'll be taking Joshua's place.'

'Him?' The old woman looked doubtful. 'He's nothing more than a boy.'

'I appreciate that, Mother. But he has hidden talents. Now, hurry and fetch us food and a tankard of ale. My belly feels as though my throat's been cut.'

Fifteen

Tom sat at a grubby wooden table in a filthy, windowless kitchen and picked half-heartedly at a tin plate of cold meat that the old woman had found for him. Opposite him, The Doctor was devouring a much bigger portion with evident relish, tearing wolfishly at the meat with his yellow teeth and washing it down with great swigs of ale from a pewter tankard. Occasionally he paused to let out an appreciative belch.

Meanwhile, 'Mother' sat at the end of the table, observing the two of them in silence. She didn't seem to want any food herself but instead chose to drink cup after cup of a colourless liquid, which she kept topping up from a bottle at her side. She was in a bad mood, judging by the sour look on her wizened face. Eventually, she spoke.

'I don't know why you've brought us another mouth to feed,' she said, her voice slurred, as though half asleep. 'It's all we can do to put meat on our own table. And where's he going to sleep?'

'We'll find somewhere for him,' said The Doctor, as though it was of little importance. 'And you know I need a good stickman. Joshua isn't going to pull through; I'm sure of that.'

She scowled. 'I never liked him anyway,' she said flatly. 'He always thought he was too good for us. And he ate too much.' She studied her son for a moment. 'How much did we earn today?' she asked.

The Doctor wiped his mouth on the sleeve of his shirt and shook his head.

'Nothing,' he said. 'In fact, I had to forgo my fee in order to procure the services of young Tom here.'

'What?' She looked horrified. 'But I thought they said you'd get five shillings a day! We have *expenses*.'

'Yes, I know . . . and chief among them are the bottles of gin you put away every night.'

She gave him a crestfallen look. 'It's medicinal,' she told him. 'It's the only thing that settles my rheumatism.'

He scowled. 'The amount you drink, it's a wonder you can stay upright,' he said. 'Anyway, don't worry about the money; if everything works out as I hope it will, this boy is going to pay his way many times over. We'll be out of this stink-hole and installed somewhere more appropriate to a man of my calibre.' He chuckled and withdrew the pack of antibiotics from his pocket. He placed them on the table in front of her. 'What do you make of those little beauties?'

'What are they?' she asked, turning the pack around in her liver-spotted hands. She opened the packet and pulled out the contents, then sniffed at them, as though that might give her a clue. 'Some kind of food?' she muttered.

'They're Sassenach pills,' said The Doctor.

'Never heard of 'em,' said Mother, scathingly.

'Neither had I until yesterday. But they can cure the plague.'

Mother stared at him. 'Could such a thing be possible?' she asked him.

'Aye. And I've seen the proof.' He took another swig from his tankard. 'The good news is that Tom here can get more of them. Hundreds.'

'I never said anything about *hundreds*,' said Tom warily, but The Doctor waved him to silence.

'He's friends with the man who invented them. All it needs is a word from him and they'll be ours.'

Mother's eyes widened in realisation. 'But . . . if you have a cure, then that means . . .'

'Aye, Mother. When I get my hands on those pills, I'll be the most sought-after man in Edinburgh! We'll make our fortunes from this. You just see if we don't.'

'I thought you were doing pretty well already,' said Tom, remembering what he had been told by Agnes Chambers. 'Aren't you being paid a small fortune to look after the plague victims?'

They both turned to look at Tom in surprise; then the old woman's mouth curled into a grin, displaying a few rotten stumps of teeth. 'Hah! He thinks you're–'

'Wheesht, woman!' interrupted The Doctor, giving her a warning glare. Then he turned to Tom. 'I've already told you to keep yer snout out of things that dinnae concern you. What I get paid for an honest day's work is my business and nobody else's. Do you understand?'

Tom bowed his head obediently but he was already putting two and two together. It hadn't felt right since he'd stepped into this place. This wasn't the big, fancy town house that both Missie Grierson and Cameron had described; what respectable doctor would be content to live in a grubby, rat-trap like this? The more Tom thought about it, the more it made sense. The Doctor never went anywhere without the leather mask and cloak – it could be anybody under there and who'd know? He thought too, about the other coach they'd met on the way here . . . the furtive man handing over a list of names. Maybe at the height of the outbreak there were just too many patients for one doctor to attend to. Maybe the real Doctor Rae was farming cases out to other people . . . or maybe . . . maybe he didn't even know that this was going on.

Now Tom remembered something else that Cameron had said. When he'd got to The Doctor's house that night, a man had been waiting for him by the gate. He'd said that The Doctor was out on a call and he'd taken the address of the orphanage and promised that The Doctor would pay a visit the following day. What's more, when he'd turned up, he'd demanded a tip of ten shillings, something that had come as a complete surprise to Missie Grierson. Now it all seemed so obvious. It was a scam. The real Doctor Rae didn't have a clue that an imposter was siphoning off some of his cases and charging for his visits.

'Hurry up and finish your food,' snapped The Doctor. 'We have more cases to attend this afternoon and I want to write a letter before we go.'

Tom obediently shoved the last few pieces of gristle into his mouth and chewed automatically. As soon as the last scrap was gone from the plate, Mother whipped it away from him and took it across the kitchen to stack with a pile of other unwashed dishes.

'Right,' said The Doctor, rubbing his greasy hands together. 'Mother, fetch writing materials. Tom and I have a letter to compose.'

The old woman hobbled away and returned after a while with a tray that contained, amongst other things, a quill pen, ink and sheets of thick, yellow paper. Tom noticed that there was also a lit candle in what looked like a gold holder, a touch that seemed oddly out of place in this setting. There was also a short stick of something red that looked like a child's crayon. The Doctor selected a sheet of paper and set it out in front of Tom on the grubby table.

'You write, I'll dictate,' he said.

Tom glanced at him, slyly. 'Wouldn't it be better if the letter came from you?' he asked.

'Er . . . no, that's all right, I'll just sign it,' said The Doctor.

'Why not write it as well?' persisted Tom. 'I'm sure a clever man like you would do a better job than I could.'

The Doctor looked irritated. 'I've already told you I have problems with my eyes,' he snapped. 'You write it and I'll sign my name to it.'

He can't write, thought Tom. *He's no more a doctor than I am!* But he dipped the quill pen into the pot of ink and prepared to do as he was told. First, The Doctor instructed him to write an address at the top of the page. Tom did the best he could with the unfamiliar quill, wishing he'd had a biro in his pocket when he'd arrived here. He managed to achieve a halting, splodgy scrawl as The Doctor dictated.

'Dear Doctor Wikepedia . . .'

'*Dear Doctor Wildebeest*,' wrote Tom. He paused for a moment, to see if The Doctor had noticed anything amiss but, though the man was watching intently as he wrote, he seemed perfectly happy with the results. Tom smiled and continued to write as The Doctor dictated, making more and more significant changes as he went on.

Dear Doctor Wildebeest,

Forgive me for writing to you in this unseemly spanner, but it has come to my detention that you may be unstable to resist me. I am Doctor George Rae, Plague Dentist and prominent sturgeon of Edinburgh. We have in our silly at this time, a most vile and headful contagion, which grows longer by the day.

Your good spend, Tom Afflick, has brought to my detention your wonderful Sausage-Pills, which have already elected a most incredible curse on a young victim of the plate. Young Tom has insured me that you would be spilling to supply me with a large quantity of these poles, which I would of course, use for the good of my patience and would ensure that they are distributed swiftly and unfairly to those moist in need of them.

I would therefore entreat you to spend at your murkiest lollipop-tunity as many sausage-pills as you can seasonably spare, in the sure and certain porridge that I, Doctor George Rae, will use them to line my own pockets.

I remain your demented serpent,

Doctor George Rae.

'Everything all right?' asked Tom innocently, handing over the sheet of paper – and The Doctor pretended to scan the page for mistakes.

'That's fine,' he said. He took the quill from Tom's hand and signed the letter with a flourish. Then he dried it with a blotter, folded it and turned it over. 'Write the doctor's address there,' he instructed, pointing.

Tom obediently wrote an address, incorporating one of the first jokes he had ever heard.

'Doctor Bob Wildebeest,
999 Letsby Avenue,
Manchester.'

'Excellent.' The Doctor picked up the red stick and held it in the flame of the candle, melting the end until a large gobbet fell onto the edges of the folded paper. As a final measure, he pressed the face of a signet ring on his third finger into the wax, leaving the impression of an eagle's head. 'There now,' he said.

He handed the envelope to his mother, who had been watching the proceedings in silence. 'Take this to the post-boy and bid him deliver it with all haste,' he told her. 'Tell him he's not to spare his horse. And whoever takes the letter to its final destination must wait for a reply before returning.' He pressed a coin into her hand. 'Give him this for his troubles,' he added.

Mother grimaced. 'A shilling? We can't afford to be handing out that kind of money,' she grumbled.

'It'll be worth it,' he assured her. 'There's civil war in England, they won't take the letter without something to put in their purse. Trust me. Up till now we've only been earning scraps. The contents of that letter will buy us the means to make a thousand shillings.'

I wouldn't hold your breath, thought Tom, with grim satisfaction.

Mother muttered something but turned and hobbled away across the room. The Doctor smiled and turned back to look at Tom. 'She's never understood,' he said. 'A man has to speculate to accumulate.' He got to his feet. 'And now we're ready to go back to work,' he said. He picked up the packet of pills and tapped them against the knuckles of one hand. 'And I think I have just the person for these little beauties,' he added. 'Come on, boy, don't sit there gawping at me. Time's a wasting and there's money to be earned!'

Tom was in the cramped interior of the carriage again, The Doctor dressed in his leather cape, as the vehicle rocked and swayed through the crowded city streets. Tom had heard The Doctor tell the coach driver that they were going to the home of Lord Kelvin, a name Tom remembered from the list given to them by the man in the other carriage and, for some reason he couldn't quite remember, a name he had seen or heard somewhere else. But first, they had stopped outside the tavern called The Four Talons, where they had collected the brazier-man, who Tom now learned was called Douglas. He was still carrying the hot brazier and had perched himself, and it, on a little shelf that stuck out from the back of the coach, where he seemed more than happy to travel.

The coach took a right turn and, after a short while, it left the crowded streets behind and moved along roads flanked by trees and fields. Peering out of the window, Tom could see a huge building ahead of them; a mansion built of grey stone and set within its own grounds.

The Doctor shook his head. 'Who would have thought

that the contagion could have found its way out to this charming place?' he murmured. He lifted the leather helmet and lowered it carefully over his face. 'You will announce me,' he told Tom, his muffled voice back to its familiar croak.

The carriage rattled along a gravelled drive and passed through some high, stone gates. As it pulled to a halt in front of the house, the front door opened and a woman hurried out to meet them. She was wearing a frilly hat and apron, rather like the ones worn by Agnes Chambers back at Mary King's Close.

As Tom climbed down from the carriage, he noticed that each of the huge windows overlooking the drive had a white sheet draped in it. The Doctor alighted too and Douglas climbed down from the back of the coach and grabbed the slumbering brazier. The woman curtsied respectfully as they approached, and waited for somebody to speak. Tom stepped forward, trying to remember the words that Joshua had used before.

'Er . . . I am Tom . . . assistant to Doctor Rae,' he said.

The woman bowed her head. 'If you will follow me, gentlemen, the master of the house is waiting to talk to you,' she said.

'Delighted,' said The Doctor.

They followed the woman up a flight of white marble steps and in through huge wooden doors. They found themselves in an opulent hallway, tiled in white marble. The velvet papered walls were hung with massive oil paintings and gilt mirrors. The woman turned back to look at them and Tom tried to remember what Joshua had said next.

'Umm . . . where's the . . . victim?' he asked, but then noticed that the woman was bowing her head as somebody else came into the hallway. Tom turned his head and stared. Coming towards him was a man wearing a white powdered wig and a fancy gold jacket. As he came nearer, he nodded to Tom and forced a smile, revealing a mouthful of rotten green teeth.

Sixteen

'You!' gasped Tom. He couldn't help himself. It was the third time he'd seen the man. The first had been when he'd just arrived on Mary King's Close, the man had been grinning out at him from the open window of the carriage that had almost knocked Tom down. The second time, weirdly, he'd been standing in the kitchen of *Wagamama's* in Manchester, looking really out of place. Now here he was again, thin, anxious and, judging by his fine clothes, a very rich man.

He took a step back when Tom spoke, a look of alarm on his face. Then he looked to The Doctor as though seeking some kind of explanation.

'Mind your manners, whelp,' snarled The Doctor and brought the end of his cane down across Tom's shoulders with a force that nearly knocked him to the floor. Tom winced and stepped back, his back stinging. The Doctor moved closer to the newcomer and bowed his masked head respectfully. 'Lord Kelvin,' he said, in that familiar muffled croak. 'An honour and a privilege, Sir. I came as soon as I had word of your terrible predicament.'

Lord Kelvin waved a white handkerchief. 'Let us not stand on ceremony,' he said, in a slow, cultured voice. 'And let's have no more unpleasantness, please. I'm already living on my nerves.' It was hard to tell how old he was.

His voice seemed somehow like that of an elderly man, but the painted face could have belonged to somebody in his thirties.

'I understand,' murmured The Doctor. 'I believe it's a child that has been stricken with the contagion.'

Lord Kelvin nodded. 'My granddaughter, Annie: eight years old and the apple of her late mother's eye. Her father is away in the wars across the border and I'm a widower myself. Annie is all I have in the world.'

Annie! thought Tom. But he was quite sure this couldn't be the fabled ghost of Mary King's Close, not living here in this fancy residence. A coincidence, he supposed.

'Your daughter was also a victim?' asked The Doctor.

'Yes, but not of the plague,' said Lord Kelvin. 'Consumption took her. She died but two months ago.'

The Doctor shook his head. 'A sad story, my Lord, yet one I hear so often. When did the child first become ill?'

'Her maid tells me the sickness fell on her yesterday afternoon. It seemed to come out of nowhere. One minute she was running across the lawn, full of mischief . . . the next she was complaining of a headache and then the vomiting started.' Lord Kelvin shook his head. He stepped closer and took The Doctor's gloved hands in his own. 'You must help her, Doctor Rae. With all that's happened recently, I couldn't bear to lose Annie as well.'

'Rest assured, I will do everything in my power,' said The Doctor, and Tom almost laughed out loud at the false sincerity in his muffled voice. 'But before we go up to see her, there's something that I must broach.'

'Name it,' said Lord Kelvin.

'It's just the trifling matter of my attendance money. It's customary to tip the doctor twenty shillings . . .'

Tom glanced at him in surprise. His fee seemed to have doubled since his last visit. Obviously he tailored it to suit each customer.

'That's of no consequence.' Lord Kelvin muttered quick instructions to the maid, who curtsied and hurried away. 'Flora will have the money ready for you when you leave,' he said.

'Thank you. One hates to ask, but my expenses are very high . . .'

'Please, don't even think about it.'

'Well, in that case, perhaps you'd be good enough to show us to the patient?'

'Of course. If you will follow me, gentlemen.'

Lord Kelvin led the way up the wide marble staircase and Tom, The Doctor and Douglas, still holding the smouldering brazier in his gloved hands, went up behind him, staring in awe at their surroundings – walls festooned with rich tapestries, great glittering candelabra hanging from the ceiling. It was a far cry from Mary King's Close and Tom couldn't help himself. He had to ask.

'What do you do?' he asked Lord Kelvin.

'Do?'

'For a living, I mean. You're obviously pretty well off.'

'Shut your mouth, you impudent cub,' snarled The Doctor. 'What did I tell you about minding your manners?'

'That's quite all right,' said Lord Kelvin, holding up a hand. 'The boy's only being curious and I find his frankness refreshing.' He smiled his rotten smile at Tom. 'I don't really do anything,' he said. 'I mean, I don't work. I inherited my wealth. My father owned woollen mills and, when he died, their ownership passed to me. Once in a while I have to go and shake hands with the workers, but that's a tiresome business, so I do it as little as possible. For the rest of the time, I read and I ride horses and I paint a little, landscapes mostly, though I've no real talent for it. And in the season, of course, I go to parties.'

'That's it?' cried Tom. 'You get paid to read and go to parties?'

'Well, I suppose I'm lucky in that I am not required to work for my daily bread.' He looked at Tom with interest. 'And how, pray, does a young lad like you end up as assistant to such an eminent physician?'

'Oh . . . I just kind of fell into it,' said Tom.

They had reached the top of the stairs and now Lord Kelvin was pushing open a huge mahogany door. They stepped into a room. Tom thought about the dirty, empty bedroom in which he had found Alison and gazed around in wonder. This room was opulent, to say the least, papered in bright colours and furnished with pieces of expensive-looking furniture: a dressing table, a wardrobe and a huge gilt-framed mirror. A fine rocking horse stood off to one side, poised mid leap, its painted eyes wild, its teeth bared. At the top of the room was a huge four-poster bed, the uprights intricately carved and hung with richly embroidered drapes. They moved closer and now they could see a little girl lying in the bed, dwarfed by its size. She looked like a doll, her pale face staring at the ceiling, her blonde hair fanned out on the pillow, arms stretched to either side. She looked very weak.

'Annie, my angel, here's the doctor come to visit you,' crooned Lord Kelvin. 'He's come to see about making you better.'

Annie's blue eyes took in the approaching figure in its leather cape and birdlike hood and an expression of sheer terror came to her face.

'Grandfather, what is it? Make it go away!'

'Wheesht, child,' growled The Doctor, stepping up beside the bed. 'Let's have no fuss. I'm here to help you.' He lifted his stick and pushed her head first to one side and then to the other. Tom could see no sign of any buboes on her slender neck. Now The Doctor set down the stick and, moving closer, he pulled aside the bed covers and, with his gloved hands, clumsily unlaced the front of her gown, pulling the fabric aside. Under one arm there was a telltale red swelling.

'Ah,' he said. He nodded, stepped back from the bed and turned to look at Douglas. He indicated a window. 'Prepare the irons,' he said.

Douglas carried the slumbering brazier across the room and, setting it down, opened the window. He began to blow on the coals, coaxing the heat to rise again. The coals reddened instantly. He unslung the heavy leather pouch from his brawny shoulder, set it down on the carpet and unrolled it to reveal the collection of ugly metal implements within.

Lord Kelvin looked down at them uneasily. 'What are they for?' he murmured, lifting a handkerchief to his face.

'They are the prescribed treatment for the plague,' said

The Doctor. 'You see this swelling under her arm? It is necessary to slice it open and drain it. I will then insert a red hot poker into the wound in order to cauterise it.'

Tom couldn't see The Doctor's expression, but for some reason he imagined the man was smiling beneath the leather mask as he said these words.

It didn't seem possible that Lord Kelvin's powdered face could look any paler but suddenly, it did. Over on the bed, Annie started to cry.

The Doctor gestured to Douglas, who selected an iron and rammed it into the glowing coals. 'The treatment is robust,' continued The Doctor. 'And the child seems rather delicate. You may want to consider having a priest present before we continue. Just in case . . .'

Now tears brimmed in Lord Kelvin's eyes and made two tracks through the white powder on his face. He dabbed at them with his lace handkerchief.

'It seems so brutal,' he gasped. 'If only there were some other way . . .'

There was a long silence . . . and then The Doctor said, 'Do you know, there just might be.'

Lord Kelvin stared at him, sensing hope. 'Speak, man! Anything would be preferable to the barbaric method you're suggesting.' He waved a hand impatiently. 'Could you not remove the mask? It's hard to converse, when . . .'

The Doctor shook his head. 'The mask must stay on,' he said. 'Too much risk of infection if I remove it.' He came closer to Lord Kelvin, as though to confide a secret. 'Are you familiar with the work of the eminent English physician, Doctor Wikepedia?' he asked.

Tom would have laughed if the situation weren't so tense.

Lord Kelvin shook his head. 'I must confess, I'm not,' he said.

'He's made some truly amazing discoveries. It's hard to believe, but he has created a pill that can cure the plague. Incredible but true! My young assistant, Tom, has worked with the man. Indeed, when he arrived here from Manchester, he brought with him a sample of those very pills, which he was kind enough to give to me. I have already used them to successfully cure other cases, right here in Edinburgh.'

Tom noticed he didn't mention that it was just the one case.

'Then let us try that!' cried Lord Kelvin. 'Pills, you say? That's the extent of the treatment?'

'It is not as straightforward as you might suppose,' said The Doctor. 'I have but one course of the pills left. Indeed, I have this very day written to Doctor Wikepedia, asking for more but, with the situation across the border, the Civil War and everything, well, it could be some time before I am in possession of them. Two or three weeks, perhaps a month.' He gestured towards the little girl in the big bed. 'I fear Annie cannot afford to wait that long.'

In that moment Tom realised just how evil a person The Doctor was. He was callously preparing his victim to demand money. Tom felt like running across the room and attacking him with every ounce of strength in his body. But he could only watch, aghast, as the hideous game unfolded.

'Then . . . I do not understand,' said Lord Kelvin. 'Why not let Annie have the pills that are already in your possession?'

'Would that I could, my Lord, but . . . this is difficult for me. You see, I have another patient, a Lady who has also contracted the contagion. Her husband is a man of means, like yourself . . . forgive me, I am not at liberty to reveal his name, but he would be well known to you. He begged me to save the life of his beloved wife and, when I told him that I had but the one dose left and that it really should go to the most deserving case, he assured me that he was willing to pay a considerable sum of money to secure it.'

'How much money?' asked Lord Kelvin, without hesitation. 'Whatever it is, I shall double it!'

Another long pause. Tom could imagine The Doctor's devious mind, clicking away as he tried to figure out just how much he could make on this.

'The other gentleman . . .'

'Yes?'

'He has promised me five hundred Scottish pounds.'

'Then, by God, you shall have a thousand! This is the life of a young child we're talking about. Of course, I'm sorry for the other lady, but she, at least, has lived her life. My granddaughter is only eight years old. I shall write you a note to my bank before you leave here.'

'Ah . . . that would be . . . inconvenient,' said The Doctor. 'I would rather be paid in cash, if that's all the same to you.'

'Cash?' For the first time, Lord Kelvin looked suspicious. 'That's a large sum of money to procure in cash, Doctor Rae.'

'I know it. But it's a delicate matter, you see. Because of my position with the City Council. If they were to become aware of such a transaction, it might be . . . awkward for me, do you understand? Doctor Wikepedia's techniques are far beyond their ken. They might not approve of me using them. So, such a payment, if 'twere made, would have to be . . . untraceable.'

Lord Kelvin nodded. He seemed reassured. 'I appreciate your position,' said Lord Kelvin. 'Cash it shall be, Doctor. I will go into the city this very day and withdraw such a sum. I'll tell them it's to purchase art. I often spend money on paintings. And I shall have it here by tomorrow morning. I would however, stipulate one condition . . .'

'Yes, Lord Kelvin?'

'Before I part with the money, I would want to be assured that my granddaughter was completely healed of the contagion. I do not intend to pay out that kind of sum on mere conjecture.'

'I quite understand. Rest assured, I shall visit every day until it is clear that Annie is out of harm's way. There are also a few other things that I would strongly advise you to do in order to give her every opportunity to recuperate.'

'Whatever you think, Doctor.'

'The girl should be washed from head to foot with lye soap and her nightdress and bedding changed for fresh ones. And if you could procure some bunches of lavender?'

'Lavender?'

'Aye. Festoon them around the bed once everything has been cleaned. It will help to ensure that there is no re-infection.'

Tom bunched his hands into fists. The Doctor was acting as though this was something he'd done before but he hadn't even seen it used until Tom had visited Alison. Tom felt like telling Lord Kelvin about the deceit, but he didn't dare speak out. The Doctor was a violent man and would doubtless thrash him, maybe something even worse, once they were away from here. Tom could only watch in disgust as The Doctor took the packet of tablets from his pocket and handed them to Lord Kelvin.

'Annie is to have one of these every morning and one at night – it's written on the box here – and she's to keep doing so until all the pills are gone. Entrust nobody else with this task, Lord Kelvin – these pills are more precious than diamonds.'

Lord Kelvin nodded. 'I shall see to it personally,' he said.

The Doctor looked at Douglas. 'Put away the irons,' he said, 'we'll no' be needing them today.'

The look on Douglas' potato-like face was one of disappointment. This was the second time he'd prepared for such a treatment only to have it cancelled on him. With no water to quench the iron, he left it in the coals and proceeded to wrap up the other instruments.

Lord Kelvin was looking at the packet doubtfully. 'It's hard to believe that it could be so easy,' he said.

'Then prepare to be astonished,' said The Doctor. 'As I was, the first time I witnessed this miracle.' He turned away. 'And now, if you will forgive my haste, we must away to my other patients. People who must endure more robust cures than young Annie. I bid you good day, Lord Kelvin – and I shall call on you tomorrow to see how things are progressing.' He looked at Tom and Douglas. 'Come along,' he said. 'We've tarried long enough and there's yet more work to be done!'

SEVENTEEN

Back in the coach, The Doctor removed his mask to reveal Hamish's sweating but delighted features. He took a leather purse from his cloak and shook the contents out into a gloved hand.

'Twenty shillings!' he exclaimed, delightedly. 'Twenty shillings for nothing more than a bit of play-acting! And a thousand pounds to follow. I'll be a wealthy man yet!'

Tom studied him in disgust. 'You're pretty pleased with yourself, aren't you?' he observed.

The Doctor's smile vanished instantly. 'What if I am?' he snarled. 'What's it to you?'

'Well, for one thing,' said Tom, 'by rights, half of that money should be mine.'

The Doctor laughed dismissively. 'How do you make that out?' he cried.

'If it wasn't for me, you wouldn't even have the pills. You wouldn't know about the clean bedding and the lavender and . . . you wouldn't have even heard of Doctor Wikepedia.'

The Doctor scowled. 'But I have the expense of housing and feeding you,' he replied. 'Not to mention the valuable apprenticeship you'll be getting.'

Tom sneered. 'An apprenticeship in how to blackmail people,' he said, 'Oh, don't worry,' he added, 'I don't want any of the money, not when it's been ripped off like that.'

'Ripped ... off?' The Doctor looked confused. It clearly wasn't a term he was familiar with.

'Yeah. I think it's disgusting what you just did to that poor bloke. OK, so he's rich, but charging him for pills that cost you nothing in the first place, that's really scuzzy. And making up that other case, so you could drive up the price?'

The Doctor fixed him with a look. 'What makes you think I made it up?' he growled.

'Oh, please! Don't even try to lie about it. Nobody else knows you've got the pills. If you're the real Doctor Rae, I'll eat my shorts. You're just some scally trying to pull a fast one.'

The Doctor returned the coins to his purse and carefully replaced it in his pocket. 'What's a scally?' he murmured.

'It's a crook, a lowlife, a scumbucket,' snarled Tom.

'And that's what you think I am?'

'Yes,' said Tom, 'and–'

That was as far as he got. The next moment, The Doctor flung himself across the narrow space between them and had Tom by the throat. He was pinning him back against the seat while he stared into Tom's face, his eyes inches away, his vile breath gusting into Tom's nostrils.

'Now you listen to me,' he said, 'and you listen good. If I ever hear you say anything like that again, if you so much as look at me the wrong way, I swear I will snap your neck like a twig, do you hear me? I don't want you talking to people, asking questions. From now on, you're my assistant, and you'll do exactly what you're told and nothing else. Do I make myself clear?'

Tom struggled to escape but the hands around his neck were pressing with incredible force, choking the very life out of him. His head was filling with a horrible buzzing red mist.

'And you'd better pray, boy, that your doctor friend in England sends me some of those pills soon, because, if the weeks go by and they don't arrive, then you'll be no use to me and, if that happens . . .'

The Doctor's stinking mouth continued to shape words but Tom could no longer hear them, because he was melting, he was running through The Doctor's gloved hands like hot sealing wax and, quite suddenly, he was no longer in the swaying interior of the coach, he was sitting in a different kind of coach altogether, the one that was taking him on the school trip to Mary King's Close. It was no longer The Doctor's face that was pushed up against his, but the fat, grinning features of his arch enemy, Stuart Gillies. The boy's big hands had hold of the lapels of Tom's blazer and he was pulling him up close, blasting the stench of half-digested cheese and onion crisps into his face.

'Say it!' he bellowed.

Tom stared back at him in bewilderment. 'Say what?' he gasped.

'Say 'I'm a waste of space!''

There was a pause while Tom tried to get his fuddled senses around the command. Part of his mind was still back in the coach with The Doctor and when he spoke, he did so without thinking it through. 'You're a waste of space!' he stammered.

A concerted 'Oooh' went up from the seats all around him and some laughter too. The response must have shocked Gillies because he let go of Tom's lapels and reeled back in surprise, the look on his face suggesting that this was the last thing he had expected. 'You trying to be funny, Manky?' he snarled.

'No, I . . . I thought that's what you wanted me to say.'

Laughter now, from the surrounding seats. Gillies glanced quickly around, sensing that his authority was slipping. 'Oh, so you're a comedian now, are you? We'll see if you're still laughing after the visit.' He threw a quick glance over his shoulder to where Mr McKenzie sat at the front of the coach, his gaze fixed on the way ahead. Gillies turned back and shoved a grubby index finger in Tom's face. 'You and me, Manky,' murmured Gillies. 'One-to-one. I'll be waiting for you.'

And, with that, he gave Tom a contemptuous shove and went back to his cronies at the back of the bus.

Tom slumped miserably against the rain-spattered window and stared out at the grey streets of Edinburgh. He wondered if he was back for good this time. If so, he had jumped backwards in time maybe only half an hour . . . at least, he told himself, he would be forewarned about what might happen at Mary King's Close . . . and, if he should happen to see a flickery vision of Morag, moving past an open doorway, there was no way he was going to be dumb enough to follow her into that room a second time. After all, although this was a reality he hated, it was also one that he recognised. Maybe his trips to the seventeenth century were over with.

'Why do you let him treat you like that?' asked a female voice.

'Huh?' He looked up in surprise to see that a girl, sitting in the seat in front of him, had turned around to look at him. She was pretty, Tom thought, with steely grey eyes and dark, shoulder-length hair. There was also something strangely familiar about her, but he couldn't think from where. He was fairly sure he hadn't spotted her in school before.

'Well?' she prompted him. 'Nothing to say for yourself?'

'Er . . . no. Sorry.' He shrugged his shoulders. 'I don't know,' he said.

'You don't know?' She seemed puzzled by this answer. 'Seems to me you should have an idea about it. Is it because you're afraid of him?'

'No, it's not that, exactly, it's just . . . look, sorry, do I know you?'

'Of course you do,' she said. 'I'm Shona. I'm in your class.'

'Er . . . OK, but I . . . I can't help feeling I've met you somewhere before. I mean, not here. Somewhere else. You . . . you haven't ever lived in Manchester, have you?'

'No, worse luck. I bet Manchester is a cool place to live. All that great music . . . and Coronation Street! Have you ever been?'

Tom shook his head. 'I don't think it's a real place,' he said.

She rolled her eyes. 'You don't say! It's a TV programme, right? Some of it must be filmed on location. I thought maybe you might have gone on a tour or something.'

'No, sorry. Not a fan.'

She shrugged. 'That's OK; it's not a test.' She smiled. 'Question is, what made you want to leave Manchester and come and live in Edinburgh?'

'Don't you know?' asked Tom. 'Everybody else seems to. My mum ran off with this guy and he lives here.' He jerked a thumb over his shoulder in the general direction of the back seat. 'They're all talking about it.'

'I don't take much notice of what they say,' said Shona, dismissively. 'They're idiots. Anyway, about Stuart Gillies. You shouldn't let him push you around like that. He's a bully. And when you stand up to a bully, he just melts away like a snowflake in a microwave.'

'It's not just him though, is it?' argued Tom. 'He's got all his mates to back him up.'

She laughed at that. 'What planet are you from?' she asked him. 'Everybody knows that kids who hang around with a bully only do it so they don't get bullied themselves. Once they see you stand up to him, they'll lose interest.'

'Think so?'

'Know so.' She smiled and, once again, he was struck by the look in those steely grey eyes. It was maddening. He was sure he knew her from somewhere. He decided to start fishing for more information.

'Are you from round here?' he asked her.

'I live on the Close,' she said.

He stared at her. 'Mary King's Close?'

'No, you bampot! Nobody lives there any more. I'm talking about Argyle Close. There's quite a few of us from there . . .' She stared at him. 'What's wrong?' she asked him.

'Bampot,' he echoed. 'You . . . called me bampot.'

'It's just something people say,' she assured him. 'Don't take it personal.'

But an idea was forming in his mind – something incredible – something he could never have anticipated; the more he looked at Shona, the more he began to place those grey eyes in an entirely different environment. 'What . . . what's your surname?' he asked her, hardly daring to breathe.

'It's Grierson,' she said. 'Why?'

He nodded. Somehow he'd known it would be. He looked at the pretty girl and tried to work out how she might change through years of hard work and hard living. He tried to imagine her with ample curves and brawny shoulders and a clay pipe jutting out of her mouth.

'Do they ever call you Missie?' he asked.

She was delighted by the question. 'How did you know that?' she cried. 'That's what my Ma and Da used to call me when I was a bairn. They used to say I was a proper little madam, whatever that means.'

'What do they call you now?' he asked her.

'This may come as a surprise to you,' she said. 'But they call me Shona.'

Gillies' voice sounded from the back seat. 'Hey, don't look now, Manky's got himself a girlfriend.'

'That's more than you've ever had,' said Shona, contemptuously, and laughter erupted from the back of the bus.

Tom glanced over his shoulder and saw that Gillies was getting up out of his seat, a vengeful expression on his face.

'Sit down, Gillies!' roared Mr McKenzie from the front of the coach and the boy reluctantly obeyed the command, but he mouthed the words 'just you wait' at Tom, before drawing his index finger across his throat. Tom turned back to look at Shona.

'Ignore that,' she told him. 'That's just show for his cronies. Shall I tell you something about Stuart Gillies?' She leaned closer. 'He still sleeps with the blanket he had when he was a wee baby . . . and, when nobody's looking, he still sucks his thumb.'

'No way!' said Tom. 'Who told you that?'

'My Ma's friends with his Ma. She's dead worried about it. Taken him to see a child psychologist and all that.' She threw a contemptuous look down the length of the bus. 'So, you see, he's the last person in the world you should be scared of. He has his own problems.'

The coach slowed and Tom saw that it was coming to a halt at St Giles Cathedral, the drop off point. Everybody jumped to their feet and started jostling for position but Mr McKenzie was there before them.

'Sit down everyone!' he yelled. 'We're going to do this in an orderly fashion. That means we'll exit the coach from the front to the back.' A groan went up from the back seat but Mr McKenzie ignored it. 'Now, let's begin, shall we? Anybody who pushes in will get right back on the coach and will stay there until the tour is finished. I hope I make myself clear.'

The threat worked. The exit was indeed orderly, and Tom soon found himself moving along the aisle, directly behind Shona, marvelling as he did so at the trimness of her figure and wondering how she could ever have ballooned up into the hulking shape of Missie Grierson. Except that didn't make sense anyway, because Missie Grierson belonged in the past, not the future. But then, there was no mistaking those eyes and that voice. They reached the door of the coach and Shona went down the steps to the cobbled road. Tom followed and the class began the walk down the Royal Mile towards Mary King's Close.

And then everything seemed to ripple and shudder and a roaring sound filled Tom's ears. His movement along the street accelerated as though he were in a film that had suddenly been switched to fast forward. Everything around him turned into a blur, making him feel sick and dizzy. He was only dimly aware of stepping in off the busy street and moving frantically around the gift shop, before following Agnes Chambers down the stairs into the darkness. Then he was lurching up and down hills as he ran like an idiot behind the other kids, moving in and out of rooms, standing in front of mad waxworks before racing on again. Then quite suddenly, everything jerked abruptly to a halt.

He was standing with the other kids in the dark, silent tomb of the Close, looking at Agnes Chambers as she said, 'That concludes our tour for today. If you'd like to follow me, we'll head back to the surface.'

Tom stood there feeling vaguely stunned. He felt like complaining. He hadn't seen *any* of the tour! He looked around for Shona, but he couldn't see her amongst the others and he began to wonder if she even existed. Agnes indicated a doorway and led the way through it and up a flight of stairs. The class followed her in polite single file. Mr McKenzie went up towards the middle of the group, urging those behind him to watch their step and to hold on to the wooden handrail. As usual, Tom hung back until the end, wanting to keep a distance between himself and the other kids. He wondered if he was back in Edinburgh for good this time. After the frantic dash he had just endured, everything seemed normal.

He went to follow the others through the doorway but a hand came out of the darkness and pushed him hard in the chest, making him reel back a step or two. His first thought was that The Doctor had somehow managed to pursue him across time, but then he saw the fat, smiling face of his enemy, Stuart Gillies stepping out of the shadows, followed by two of his cronies.

'Aren't you forgetting something, Manky?' he asked. 'You and me have some business to settle before we head back to school.'

Eighteen

Tom shook his head as he realised that even here, in the real world, trouble was hard to evade. But at the same time, he felt incredibly relieved. After all, Gillies was just a bully. Stand up to him and he'd melt away like a snowflake in a microwave. Or at least, that's what Shona had told him.

'What's the matter, Manky?' asked Gillies mockingly. 'You look scared.'

'I'm not,' Tom told him, and was vaguely surprised to realise that this was absolutely true. After everything he'd been through in the seventeenth century, Gillies and his pathetic friends didn't bother him one little bit. 'I'd need a reason to be scared, wouldn't I?' he said. 'And you're just pathetic.'

Gillies was surprised enough to take a step backwards. 'You . . . what did you say?'

'What's the matter?' asked Tom. 'Hard of hearing? If you think I'm scared of a total loser like you then think again.' He paused for a moment then smiled. 'I have to congratulate you though.'

'On what?' grunted Gillies, looking completely baffled.

'On coming all the way down to this dark, spooky place without your special blanket.'

Gillies reddened. 'What . . . what are you talking about?' he snarled.

'Oh, don't your mates *know* about that?' asked Tom, innocently. He turned to look at the cronies, who had stopped grinning and were now looking uncertain. 'Stuart has this little blanket; he's had it since he was a baby. He can't go to sleep without it.'

Gillies looked horrified. 'That's not true!' he protested.

'Oh, but it is, Stuart. Have you never told your mates about it?'

Gillies pushed Tom hard in the chest. 'Shut up!' he cried.

'Oh yeah, I nearly forgot.' Tom grinned maliciously. 'He sucks his thumb too. His mum's dead worried about it. Taken him to see a doctor and everything.'

Gillie's chubby face was now crimson. 'I told you to shut up!' he cried. He rushed forward and threw a wild punch at Tom's face, but he ducked easily under it, grabbed the extended arm and twisted it around behind Gillies' back. Then he pulled hard upwards and Gillies gave a kind of yelp, before dropping to his knees with a bellow of pain. Tom leaned closer to speak directly into Gillies' ear. 'Tell them it's true.'

'Will not,' grunted Gillies, so Tom pulled harder on the arm. He glanced around at Gillies' comrades but not one of them was making a move to help him. They were just standing there, open-mouthed.

'Say it,' snarled Tom.

Gillies shook his head defiantly

'Say it!' repeated Tom, increasing the pressure. 'Tell them what you do.'

'I . . . I sleep with a special blanket,' whispered Gillies.

'Louder!'

'I sleep with a special blanket!'

'Good. And what else?'

'Please, I . . .'

'SAY IT!'

'I suck ma thumb!'

'Good,' said Tom. 'Well done.' He released Gillies' arm and put a foot against his back and pushed forward. Gillies collapsed face down on the floor, blubbering, then rolled over onto his back. Tom looked around at the others. 'Anyone else?' he asked brightly. There were no takers. They were all staring down at Gillies in dismay.

'Right then,' said Tom. He stared down at Gillies, who looked somehow pathetic, and he actually felt a wave of pity for the boy, to be so humiliated in front of his friends. Against all his better judgement, Tom reached out a hand to help him to his feet. Gillies shook his head at first, but Tom kept his hand there and after a few moments Gillies gave in and reached up to accept help . . . but the hand that clamped itself around Tom's hand was not Gillies' hand. It was gloved and it was pulling at him with incredible power, yanking him clean off his feet and down onto the ground.

He rolled onto his back and peered up into darkness, expecting to see the stone roof of the Close above him – but somehow he was back in the open air. It was night time and a handful of stars twinkled in the narrow strip of black sky beyond the rooftops. He was lying on the cobbled street again, beside the coach in which, only a few minutes earlier, or so it seemed, The Doctor had been strangling the life out of him. But that had happened in broad daylight and now it was dark, so hours must have passed since then. Tom felt bone-tired and thirsty, and badly in need of a hot bath – and, now he thought of it – his clothes seemed to have an unpleasant smoky smell about them. He lay there, confused, trying to remember, and The Doctor's unmasked face moved into view, gazing down at him without a shred of pity.

'Get up,' he said, in the croaking voice that Tom had already learned to despise. 'You were next to useless. You'll do better tomorrow or you'll suffer the consequences.'

Tom stumbled wearily upright to see that Douglas was approaching from the rear of the coach, still carrying the ever-present brazier, the coals now burned out. He set it down for a moment.

'Good work today, Douglas,' said The Doctor, pressing a coin into his hand.

Douglas nodded, but he seemed worried. 'Thank you, sir,' he said. 'Begging your pardon, sir, but I'm not sure the boy's cut out to be a stickman. It's a hard enough task for a grown man, let alone a youngster.'

'You let me worry about that,' The Doctor advised him. 'Practice makes perfect and we'll make a stickman of him yet. I'll see you tomorrow at the Four Talons, the usual time.'

'Very good, sir.' Douglas picked up his brazier and trudged away, evidently reluctant to push his employer any further on the subject. Tom wondered what The Doctor had made him do while he was 'gone' and was also relieved that he didn't seem to remember any of it. The stickman, he knew, was the man who handled the hot poker. Even the thought of it made him feel queasy. Had he been made to cauterise buboes on other less affluent victims of the plague? He hoped not, but the smell of his clothes suggested otherwise.

'Right,' said The Doctor. He flicked a coin up to the coachman with familiar ease. 'Pick me up tomorrow morning at eight.' The coachman nodded and cracked his whip above the heads of his horses. They lurched forward and the coach rattled away along the cobbled street. The Doctor grabbed Tom's collar and frogmarched him towards the big, dark outline of his house. Through a soot-grimed window, in the dim glow of an oil lamp, Tom could see Mother's glum features staring hopefully out into the night. The Doctor threw open the door and strode into the hallway, pushing Tom ahead of him.

'Mother!' he roared. 'I am returned with great news. Today has been a red letter day!'

She came shuffling out into the hallway, holding the lantern in front of her. 'I thought I heard a coach,' she observed. 'You're late.' Tom could tell from her voice that she'd been drinking again.

'Aye,' said The Doctor, pulling off his leather cape and hanging it on its peg. 'There were three cases of contagion in the Close to deal with before I could even think about getting away. And yon one was no great shakes with a hot poker, neither.' He pointed at Tom. 'Couldn't stop his hands from trembling.'

Mother threw Tom a contemptuous look, and shook

her head as though there was no hope for him. 'I told you he was dead weight,' she said.

'Never mind that!' said The Doctor. 'Wait till you see how well I've done for us.' They went through into the kitchen. The Doctor pulled a bulging purse from his pocket and slammed it down onto the table. 'There's fifty shillings to begin with,' he announced.

Fifty? Tom did the simple sum in his head. So that was twenty from Lord Kelvin and ten from each of the other three patients. Not a bad day's haul for somebody who wasn't even a real doctor.

Mother set down the lantern on the table and opened the drawstring of the purse, as though she didn't believe him. She shook some coins out onto her hand and rattled them between her fingers. 'Fifty shillings,' she murmured. 'Of course, we'll have to give a share of this to McLeish, but even so, that's . . .'

'Nothing,' interrupted The Doctor, triumphantly. 'A mere trifle. For I have this day made an arrangement with none other than Lord Kelvin himself, to let him have the Sassenach pills for the sum of . . . one thousand Scottish pounds.'

Mother let out a gasp and sat down heavily in a chair. 'No!' she cried. 'You're jesting with me!' She reached for her mug and gulped down a mouthful of gin.

'Mother, I'm telling you what happened. The money's ours just as soon as his Lordship's granddaughter recovers from the plague.'

Mother looked worried. 'She *will* recover?' she croaked.

'Of course she will, in a matter of a few days. Rest

assured. And, as it's a deal that I made without McLeish's knowledge, there'll be no need to give him a cut. It will all be ours. Think, Mother! We'll be able to leave this cesspit and take lodgings in a good house in the city. We'll have fine clothes and good food and . . . maybe even servants.'

'Servants?'

'Aye, why not? When that new consignment of pills arrives from England, we'll be set up for life!' He reached out to her, pulled her up out of the chair and the two of them danced a weird little jig of sheer delight.

Tom stood there and watched them in weary silence. He realised in that moment that although the two of them were undoubtedly evil, still, they had powerful reasons for acting the way they did. The desire to escape the awful poverty in which they were trying to survive must be the strongest motivator of all. But it didn't excuse their behaviour, not one bit. He moved to a chair and slumped in to it.

'Now,' roared The Doctor, breaking away from Mother. 'Bring food and drink. Open that good bottle of brandy I've been saving.'

'And the boy?'

'Aye, give him something. Not too much, mind. We don't want to spoil him, do we?'

Mother shuffled away to the other end of the kitchen and busied herself preparing a meal as The Doctor sat himself at the table and gloatingly counted out his coins. After a little while, he became aware of Tom watching him and he looked up.

'What are you staring at?' he muttered. 'I don't like you

looking at me.'

Tom shrugged. 'I was just thinking,' he said. 'What if your mother's right? What if Annie doesn't get better? What if she dies?'

The Doctor's eyes narrowed. 'Why would she?' he said. 'The girl at the orphanage made a full recovery.'

Tom nodded. 'That doesn't mean that Annie will,' he said. 'Antibiotics don't work for everyone, you know.'

'It will work,' said The Doctor. 'It *must* work.' He was trying to sound confident but Tom could see by his expression that he was disturbed by the idea. He glared at Tom. 'Why didn't you mention this before?'

'You never asked,' said Tom, enjoying the brief sense of power he got from messing around with The Doctor's expectations. 'I'd say they work around . . . sixty percent of the time.' He didn't know this for a fact; he was just pulling The Doctor's chain and delighting at the results.

'Sixty percent,' muttered The Doctor. 'Well, it's still better odds than the old method,' he said.

Mother shuffled to the table with a tray containing a bottle of brandy for The Doctor and a mug of scummy-looking water for Tom. The Doctor grabbed the bottle, uncorked it and took a greedy swig from its contents. He gasped and wiped his mouth on his sleeve. Tom meanwhile took a cautious sip from the mug. The water tasted vile but he was parched and needed to drink something to keep himself going. Mother also set down two tin plates of meat. The Doctor's plate was piled high, while Tom's portion was smaller than his clenched fist. He regarded it dismally. The meat was grey and rotten, what looked like the last scraps of skin and gristle, pulled from a days-old carcass. As he stared down at it, he saw something moving. He reached down gingerly with his finger and thumb and pulled out a wriggling maggot.

'Oh, that's mingin'!' he exclaimed. 'I'm not eating this.'

The Doctor stared at him. 'Oh yes you are,' he growled.

'No way!' protested Tom. 'It's got maggots in it.'

'So?' shrieked Mother. 'That's good food, that is. The best money can buy.'

'*You* eat it then,' said Tom. 'It's not fit for the pigs.'

The Doctor reacted as though Tom had just struck her. 'How dare you say that to my mother?' he said. 'You ungrateful wretch!'

Tom pointed at The Doctor's plate. 'There's nothing wriggling around in your food,' he said. 'Why don't you swap with me if it's so great?'

'Eat it,' said The Doctor, coldly, getting to his feet.

Tom shook his head. 'I'm not hungry,' he insisted. 'You can't make me.'

The Doctor came slowly around the table, his eyes burning into Tom's.

'Last time,' he said. 'Are you going to eat your food or not?'

'No,' said Tom. 'And you can't–'

The Doctor's hand was at the back of his head and he was pushed, face down, into the plate of meat. It was plastered into his eyes and up his nose. He struggled frantically, unable to breathe, while The Doctor's voice roared from somewhere behind him. 'Who do you think you are?' he bellowed. 'Coming into my house and telling my mother that her food is unfit for pigs! Think yourself lucky that I haven't taken the cane to you!'

He grabbed a handful of Tom's hair and pulled him backwards, hard, tipping up the chair and sending him sprawling onto the bare earth floor. Tom lay there, gasping for breath, wiping the stinking meat from his eyes on the sleeve of his blazer.

'Well,' said The Doctor, looming threateningly over him, 'since our guest isn't in the mood to take refreshment, I'd best show him to his quarters.' He reached down, grabbed the lapel of Tom's blazer and pulled him upright. Then he dragged him out of the kitchen and back into the hall. If Tom had expected to be shown a room, he was disappointed. The Doctor stopped at the wooden enclosure. It was filled with straw, the kind of thing where a large dog or some other animal might have slept. There was a metal-barred door across the front, which opened when The Doctor pulled at it. He flung Tom carelessly inside and slammed the bars shut again. Tom struggled to turn around, the roof too low for him to even kneel upright. He managed to twist around until his nose was up against the bars. There was a rasping sound as The Doctor slid home a bolt, somewhere that Tom couldn't see. The Doctor leaned closer, his expression one of mocking triumph.

'There now,' he said. 'I trust his Majesty will be comfortable for the night.'

'You . . . you can't keep me in here!' protested Tom. 'There . . . there are laws about this kind of thing!' He grabbed hold of the bars and shook them hard, but they held firm. 'Let me out, now!'

'What's the matter? This is very grand accommodation. This was where I used to keep Bertie, my bull mastiff. Best bear-baiting dog in Edinburgh, he was. Very valuable. You should be honoured. If that last bear hadn't been too quick for him, he'd be living here yet.'

Tom shook the bars, his eyes filling with tears. 'Let me out!' he screamed. 'Please! I'll eat the meat; I'll do whatever you tell me. Just don't leave me here.'

But The Doctor was shaking his head. 'Too late,' he said. 'Kitchen's closed. The customers weren't grateful enough for my poor mother's efforts.'

Tom started crying, pummelling his fists against the iron bars.

'And if you carry on making that racket,' added The Doctor, 'I'll be back out with my cane. And you will not enjoy that one little bit.'

With that, he turned and strode back into the kitchen, slamming the door behind him. Tom was abruptly plunged into darkness. He lay there, sobbing, alone, hoping against hope that something would happen to take him out of here, off to some other reality. No matter how crazy, no matter how dangerous, anything would be preferable to this.

But though he lay there in the stinking straw, sobbing and shaking for what felt like hours, no salvation came – and it was only much later, when the house had fallen silent, that he finally found some sleep.

Nineteen

He was standing in front of a mirror, wearing a long, leather cape. On a table beside him was The Doctor's mask, the curved beak pointing upwards. Tom looked at it for a moment, then reached out and picked it up. Lifting it, he slipped it over his own head, until the edges settled over his shoulders and he was staring through the eye holes. He stood there, gazing at his reflection and wondered why he suddenly felt so powerful, so *alive*. Behind him, he heard a clamour of voices and, turning, he saw that his class from Edinburgh, dressed in their maroon blazers, were milling in through an open doorway, staring at him in total amazement. One of the girls, Jenny, pointed at him.

'Crow Boy!' she shrieked. 'He's a Crow Boy!'

He opened his mouth to protest, to tell her she was mistaken, that he'd just been trying the outfit on for a laugh, but all that emerged from his mouth was a high-pitched, rasping shriek, the sound an angry bird would make.

Now the rest of the class joined in with Jenny, chanting the two words over and over. 'Crow Boy, Crow Boy, CROW BOY!' Their jeering faces seemed to swirl around him in a blur of colour.

Tom raised his arms to try and quieten their shouts, and his leather-clad arms dissolved into a flurry of black feathers. Then he was powering himself up into the air, hovering over the class and staring intently down at them, ready to take his revenge . . .

He woke suddenly, aware of a soft noise from somewhere nearby. He lay in a foetal position, half in, half out of the dream, breathing hard, aching in every joint because he was so cramped in the narrow confines of the cage. Darkness pressed around him like a shroud and, for a moment, he thought the sound was being made by a rat or something, snuffling at the bars of the cage. Gradually he became aware that it was the sound of somebody breathing.

'Who's there?' he murmured.

Beside him, a spark was struck, and another and finally, a bit of kindling ignited and was held to the wick of a candle. The flame burned steady and a glum face peered through the bars at him – the last face he expected to see.

'Cameron?' he whispered. 'What are you . . .?'

Cameron waved him to silence and held a finger to his lips. He moved closer to the bars. 'Keep your voice down,' he hissed. 'The Doctor's asleep in the kitchen, smashed out of his head on brandy. But I don't know what's happened to the old woman. She could be a light sleeper.'

Tom shook his head. 'But what are you doing here?' he whispered back.

Cameron frowned. 'Don't think I haven't asked myself the same question,' he murmured. 'But Morag said she'd never speak to me again if I didn't get you back and Missie Grierson . . .' Cameron frowned. 'She was not happy with me,' he concluded. 'So what choice did I have?'

He was moving the candle around the cage, trying to find how the door was secured. 'Ah,' he said, at last. 'Got it. Hold tight.' He began to pull at an unseen bolt, which let out a creaking sound that seemed incredibly loud in the dark hallway. Cameron winced and glanced around, before continuing, trying to move the bolt in small increments, so it would make less noise.

'How did you get in here?' asked Tom, still trying to get his head around what was happening.

'There's a loose window out on the street,' said Cameron with a grin. 'I was waiting when they brought you in, but I had to hang around for hours before I had a chance to try the window.' He made a final effort and the bolt came free. Cameron gently opened the barred door and Tom dragged himself out, his arms and legs clumsy with cramp. Cameron gave him an arm to lean on and they got themselves upright. 'Now,' he murmured. 'Follow me, as quiet as a mouse.'

He led Tom through an open doorway into another room at the front of the house and indicated a casement window that he had left ajar.

'This way,' he said. He set down the candle and clambered expertly through the narrow opening, then reached back to lend Tom a hand to squeeze through. It was an effort. Pins and needles were shooting through Tom's arms and legs but he somehow managed to scramble through the narrow opening and, a few moments later, he dropped to the ground and followed Cameron away from the house and along the deserted street beyond.

They walked for quite a distance before Tom spoke

again. His mind was racing. 'How did you know where to find me?' he asked.

'Saw you today on the High Street,' explained Cameron. 'I'd gone out to get vegetables from the market and I saw you and The Doctor and this other fellow with a brazier. You all got out of a coach and went off into the Close together.'

'Yeah. We sorted out some plague victims there,' said Tom. 'Or at least, I think we did. I don't remember any of it.'

Cameron sighed, shook his head. 'Well, you haven't changed,' he observed. 'You still make as much sense as a raving lunatic.'

'Thanks,' said Tom, grinning.

'Anyhow, I got talking to the coach driver, didn't I? Asked him if he always took the famous Doctor Rae around the city and he said yes, but it was funny, because the doctor never seemed to go back to his own house, but to this place off Fleshmarket Close, not the kind of house you'd expect to find a rich doctor. I asked him for the address and he said he couldn't possibly remember, but he did have a powerful thirst and maybe a tankard of ale would loosen his tongue.' Cameron scowled. 'Bloody liar,' he said, 'it took three tankards and cost me all the money I had left in the world.'

Tom looked at Cameron with new respect, realising how hard it must have been to spend those three precious pennies, all earned emptying Mr Selkirk's chamber pot. 'It was good of you to do that,' he said. 'Really, I appreciate it.'

'I hope you do,' said Cameron. 'Cos believe you me, I

thought long and hard about leaving you to it. But I didn't much like the idea of never speaking to Morag again, so . . .' He shrugged his shoulders. 'In the end, the coach driver told me where the house was, so I made my way up here and waited for you. I stood around for ages. I was just about to give up when the coach arrived and you went inside. I was watching through the window.' He glanced at Tom. 'I wouldn't say you enjoyed that dinner much.'

Tom frowned. 'Rotten bully,' he muttered. 'They're all the same. Once you stand up to them, they melt away like snowflakes in a microwave.' The words had come automatically to him and he couldn't remember where he'd heard them first. Then he remembered. Shona – the girl who was a younger version of Missie Grierson.

Cameron gave him a blank look. 'What's a microwave?' he asked.

'Never mind,' said Tom.

'Well, all right, there's something else I don't understand. Why would a great man like Doctor Rae treat somebody like that?'

'Because he *isn't* Doctor Rae,' said Tom. 'Just some crook pretending to be him. He charges all of his patients money; that's how he makes his living.'

'But how come nobody ever realises he . . .' Cameron's voice trailed away as he thought about it. 'Of course,' he said. 'It could be *anyone* behind that mask.'

Tom nodded then lifted his head at the sound of wheels clattering on cobbles. He turned and saw a coach coming slowly along the street from the other direction. He lifted a hand and hailed the coachman. The man pulled on the reins and the coach rumbled to a halt. He sat there, looking doubtfully down at the boys.

'What do you two want?' he asked them and eased back his cloak to show the pistol in his belt.

'We want to go to Lord Kelvin's house,' said Tom.

'Do we?' grunted Cameron.

'Yes, we do,' said Tom. He looked up at the coach driver. 'Do you know where that is?'

The coachman grinned. 'Aye, of course I know. He's one of the richest men in Edinburgh. Don't know about taking a couple of bairns like you there, though. Is it some kind of joke you're playing? Only I was just about to go on home for the night.'

'It's no joke,' Tom assured him. 'We need to go there now.'

'And you have money for the fare?' asked the man. 'It's quite a way.'

Tom looked hopefully at Cameron, but he shook his head. Tom pondered for a moment and then an idea came to him. He reached into the pocket of his blazer and pulled out his five pound note. He handed it up to the coachman.

'There you go,' he said.

'What's this?' asked the coachman.

'That's five English pounds,' Tom assured him.

The man grunted. 'Who's the sour-faced old biddy?'

'It's the Queen of England.'

'Henrietta? It's a poor likeness of her. I heard she was in France, hiding away from the Civil War.'

'Yeah, but don't worry, that money's good, anywhere you go. It's worth ten Scottish pounds.'

The man shook his head. 'I've no change,' he warned Tom.

'Not a problem. You can keep it. And when I've spoken to Lord Kelvin, I wouldn't be surprised if he has even more money for you.'

'You reckon?' The man looked at Tom doubtfully and then shrugged his shoulders. 'I must be going simple in my old age,' he muttered. 'All right, I suppose you'd better get in.'

Tom threw open the door and he and Cameron clambered inside. The coachman lashed the horses and they took off at speed.

'What's all this about?' demanded Cameron. 'Why are you going to see that mean old bugger?'

Tom looked at Cameron. 'Why do you say that?' he asked. 'It sounds like you know him.'

'Of course I know him. He's the one Missie Grierson sent the letter to, asking him to be patron of our orphanage. Do you not remember? You read it out, the first day you arrived on the Close.'

Tom slapped a hand against his forehead. 'Of course!' he said. 'I knew I'd heard the name somewhere before. Oh man, that's weird. Everything . . . everything seems to slot together, like a jigsaw puzzle or something.' He sat back in his seat. 'Anyway, Lord Kelvin's granddaughter has the plague and Doctor Rae . . . or whoever that guy is back at the house, he sold him my pills for a thousand pounds.'

'A thousand!' Cameron sat back in his own seat, his eyes wide. He seemed to be trying to imagine what such a vast sum of money might look like. 'But . . . they were your pills. He stole them from you. That money should be yours.'

'It's not about the money,' said Tom. 'I don't want anything for them, but I sure as hell don't want that robbing scumbag to have it, either.'

The coach raced along through the darkness. It was moving out of the city now and onto the country roads beyond. Tom leaned out of the window and stared at the way ahead but could see little, save for the dappled moonlight filtering down through a swaying canopy of trees.

Fifteen minutes later, the coach slowed as it clattered up to the main gates of Lord Kelvin's house – but the gates were closed and, as Tom and Cameron clambered down from the coach, they were met by a brawny-looking man who emerged from a small sentry box beside the gates, accompanied by a fearsome-looking dog on a length of chain.

'What's your business here at this time of night?' he demanded, his hand on the handle of a sword that hung at his side.

'Please, Sir, we need to see Lord Kelvin,' said Tom.

The man glowered at them. 'You must be joking with me!' he exclaimed. 'Go away and come back at a more respectable hour.' The dog, hearing the note of threat in the man's voice, emitted a deep growl.

'We can't,' said Tom, defiantly. 'We have to see him now.'

'Aye,' said Cameron.

The man laughed. 'If you think I'm going to wake Lord Kelvin at the behest of two snot-nosed kids, you've another think coming,' said the man. 'Now shift yourselves, before I set the dog on you.'

'This is . . .' Tom thought for a moment. 'A matter of life or death.'

'Aye,' said Cameron. 'It concerns Lord Kelvin's granddaughter.'

'Annie,' added Tom.

The man looked doubtful. 'What about her?' he muttered.

'I was here yesterday with Doctor Rae,' said Tom. 'He gave her medicine for the plague. Now he's sent me with urgent instructions. If Lord Kelvin doesn't act on them right away, his granddaughter could die.'

The unexpected sound of a whiplash made them all jump. The coach lurched around in a tight circle and headed back the way it had come. Clearly, the very mention of the word 'plague' had persuaded the driver to make a hasty exit. Tom returned his attention to the guard.

The man swallowed and Tom saw that his expression had changed to one of fear. Tom could imagine what was going through his mind. Did he really want to risk being responsible for the death of Lord Kelvin's granddaughter? After a few moments, he seemed to come to a decision. He removed a big ring of keys from his belt and unlatched the gate. Then he ushered Tom and Cameron inside and he and the dog followed. 'This had better be genuine,' he warned them.

'It is,' Tom assured him. They strode along the drive and up to the front door. Tom pounded the brass knocker, the noise of it seeming to reverberate throughout the silent house. They waited. After what seemed an age, the glow of an oil lamp showed through one of the glass panes and the maid appeared at the door, dressed in her nightgown. She took some convincing before she finally agreed to go and wake 'the Master.'

Tom and Cameron were shown into the library – a huge room, the walls of which were lined with shelves filled with leather-bound books. Tom took it in his stride, but Cameron kept gazing around in awed amazement as though he'd never seen anything like it in his life – which, Tom reflected, he probably hadn't. More time passed, slowly, maddeningly, before the door opened and Lord Kelvin came into the room, wearing what looked like a silk dressing gown. His wig was gone and he was wearing a nightcap with a long tassel hanging over his shoulder. Without the powder and rouge on his face, it was plain that he was, indeed, much older than Tom had imagined, his face lined and wrinkled. He stared at the two boys in indignation.

'What's the meaning of this?' he inquired. 'And what's so important that it can't wait until morning?' He focused on Tom. 'Aren't you the boy that called here earlier today? With Doctor Rae?'

Tom nodded. 'That was me,' he agreed. 'But it *wasn't* Doctor Rae.' He motioned to an empty seat. 'If you'd like to sit down, Sir, I'll tell you everything I know.'

TWENTY

When Tom finally finished talking, the first rays of morning sunlight were filtering through the library window. Tom hadn't mentioned anything about time travel – he figured that would be pushing his luck. His story had started with him arriving in the Close from Manchester, but he hadn't said anything about his method of transport. Lord Kelvin sat there, studying his hands, which were clasped in his lap. He seemed to be deciding whether or not to actually believe Tom's story.

'Incredible,' he muttered, at last. 'Absolutely incredible.' He reached out to a brass bell that stood on a nearby table and rang it, the noise so shrill that it made Tom flinch.

After a few moments, Millie, now dressed in her uniform, bustled into the room. 'You called, my Lord?'

'Yes, Millie. I wish you to instruct McTavish to take my coach and go forthwith to the Constable's Lodge on Edinburgh High Street. Tell him to ask for Captain Dalglish and to request that he send two of his best men to me directly. Tell him to be sure they are burly fellows because they will be required to apprehend a villain.'

Millie raised her eyebrows. 'Very good, my Lord,' she said and hurried out of the room. Lord Kelvin returned his attention to the boys. He looked troubled. 'So, am I to take it that the pills this so-called Doctor left me are also a lie? Only, I had thought that Annie seemed a little more settled last night.'

'Oh no, the pills are good,' Tom assured him. 'They really should work.'

'And this Doctor Wikepedia you mentioned. He will send more?'

Tom shook his head. 'There's no such person,' he admitted. 'I made him up to keep The Doctor off my back. I'm sorry, but there's no way of getting any more. I really wish I could help.'

Lord Kelvin frowned. 'But they must have originated from *somewhere*,' he insisted. 'Think what wonders we could achieve here in Edinburgh, if we had more of them. Would you have any idea what the ingredients are?'

Tom could only shrug his shoulders helplessly. 'I'm sorry,' he said again. 'I really haven't a clue.'

'And if we were to send you back to Manchester, could you not lay your hands on more of them?'

Tom shook his head. It was hopeless. How could he tell the old man that in order to get them, he'd also have to go hundreds of years into the future? And that most of the pill's ingredients, listed on its packaging, hadn't been discovered yet. 'I'm sorry,' he said again. 'The pills that Annie has are the only ones in the world right now. I know it sounds crazy, but it's true.'

Lord Kelvin thought for a moment. 'That's a pity,' he said. 'A great pity.' He got up from his seat and walked across the study to a wooden desk which held a selection of papers and writing implements. He took a seat at it. 'The orphanage you spoke of,' he said. 'Mrs Grierson . . .?'

'*Missie* Grierson,' Cameron corrected him.

'Ah, yes. It seems to me that I have heard of this place before, but I can't quite recall where and when.'

'She wrote to you,' said Cameron. 'Asking you to be our patron.'

Lord Kelvin's eyes widened as he remembered. 'Ah, yes, of course,' he said. 'In my capacity as President of the Foundling's Trust!' He considered for a moment. 'Oh dear,' he said. 'I rather fear I declined her invitation.'

'Yes,' said Cameron, flatly. 'You did.'

Lord Kelvin allowed himself a twisted smile. 'I wonder,' he said, 'Would it be too late to reconsider my position?'

'Huh?' said Cameron.

'I think he's saying he's changed his mind,' said Tom excitedly.

'What, really?' asked Cameron.

Lord Kelvin nodded. 'If you two splendid boys are an example of the young men who originate from there, then I think it would be the least I could do. We might also think about finding you a home somewhere more suitable than that stinking Close.' He nodded, as though his mind was made up on the matter. 'I shall write to Missie Grierson immediately,' he said. 'Perhaps you'd be kind enough to convey my letter to her?'

Cameron grinned. 'Oh, yes, Sir,' he said. 'Thank you, Sir.'

'And while I'm about it, I think I'd better write to the *real* Doctor Rae and tell him to be a little more careful about who is hanging around his gates at night. What was the other fellow's name? The one who takes the names and addresses? McLeish, did you say?'

'Yes, Sir,' said Tom, 'I think that's his name.'

'We'll have the constables pay him a visit too, just in case he's of a mind to find a replacement for your imposter.' He picked up his pen and began to write, but then seemed to think of something else. 'I wouldn't mind betting that you boys haven't had any breakfast yet,' he said.

'No, Sir,' said Cameron. 'We're *starving*.'

Tom elbowed him in the ribs, but Lord Kelvin just grinned his rotten grin.

'Then once I've written these letters and I'm properly dressed, you shall join me for an early breakfast,' he said. 'We may as well fortify ourselves before that scoundrel turns up to claim his payment.' He smiled. 'I don't know about you two, but I've quite an appetite this morning!'

Some time later, the two boys found themselves in an opulent dining room, sitting at a long, oak table, while three liveried servants stood ready to dish up the breakfast. The table had a view of the driveway up to the front entrance.

A door opened and Lord Kelvin, dressed now in his more familiar style, and wearing his powdered wig, entered the room and took a seat at the head of the table. He gleefully told the boys that he had just called in on Annie and that she seemed much improved from last night.

'She even feels up to taking a little nourishment,' he told them. 'And, judging by the look of you, you're ready to do the same.' He gestured to the servants and they began serving the breakfast, bringing over a series of silver platters, each of them heaped with food. Tom looked at Cameron's face in sly amusement. The boy's eyes got bigger and bigger as each successive dish was brought out for his inspection and more and more food was heaped onto his plate – succulent sausages glistening with fat; thick juicy rashers of pork; fried eggs with bright yellow yolks; and dark, tangy smoked kippers – all washed down with cup after cup of hot sweet tea. Tom had forgotten how hungry he was and soon, he and Cameron were in competition to see who could devour the most food, though Tom had to admit, Cameron was winning by a mile. It seemed incredible that a boy so skinny could put away so much grub. Meanwhile, Lord Kelvin picked at his own meagre portion with all the delicacy of a bird.

'You boys seem to be enjoying your food,' he observed at one point and they could only nod in agreement, their mouths too full to comment.

As they were finishing up, a coach rattled to a halt in front of the house and Tom felt anxiety rippling through him, in case it was The Doctor, calling to visit Annie – but instead, two brawny strangers wearing frock coats and tricorn hats stepped out of the vehicle and strode purposefully to the front door. Millie ushered them into the dining room and they introduced themselves as special constables Taggart and McVeigh. Lord Kelvin invited them to sit and have some tea while they waited for The Doctor's arrival. He told them that once they had the imposter in their clutches, they were to convey him to Captain Dalglish's lock-up to await trial.

'If the scoundrel gives you any trouble, please feel free to give him a good walloping,' said Lord Kelvin, brightly.

They all settled down to wait and presently, another

coach moved into view and, sure enough, the figure that emerged this time was cloaked and hooded in leather, a white stick clutched in his gloved hands. As Tom watched him striding towards the front door, he felt a curious mingling of emotions: fear, because he knew how angry The Doctor would be when he discovered how Tom had betrayed him – and triumph, because he would be helping to finish the man's crooked career, once and for all.

Lord Kelvin told Taggart and McVeigh to stand ready and then beckoned to Tom. 'Come,' he said. 'Let's go and meet your Master.'

Tom felt apprehensive but did as he was told. He and Lord Kelvin walked out into the hallway, to find The Doctor standing with Millie. The Doctor turned to greet Lord Kelvin and saw Tom. His face of course, was hidden, but his eyes widened and Tom could imagine the look of shock that must have been there.

'What . . . what are you doing here?' he snarled. 'How dare you come here, bothering his Lordship?'

'Oh, but he's been no bother at all,' said Lord Kelvin. 'On the contrary, he's been telling me a very interesting story indeed, Doctor Rae . . . but that's not your real name, is it?'

There was a short, stunned silence before The Doctor tried to bluff it out. 'Your Lordship, I wouldn't take notice of anything this boy has to say,' he argued. 'He's a natural born liar.'

'Is that a fact?' said Lord Kelvin. 'So it's not true that you've been impersonating Doctor George Rae? Or that you stole the so-called Sassenach pills from this boy?'

'That . . . that's ridiculous!' blustered The Doctor. 'You don't want to be listening to anything he tells you.'

Tom felt a rush of resentment pulse through him. 'You're calling *me* a liar?' he cried. 'That's rich coming from you!'

'You shut your mouth!' snapped The Doctor. 'Lord Kelvin, if you would just give me a chance to explain myself . . .'

'Oh, you'll have a chance to explain, all right,' said Lord Kelvin. 'In court. Gentlemen?'

At that point, Taggart and McVeigh stepped briskly out from cover. Before The Doctor could even think about making a run for it, they were standing on either side of him, each of them clutching an arm.

'Take your hands off me!' he roared. 'Do you know who I am?'

'No, we don't,' said Lord Kelvin. 'Let's have a wee look, shall we?'

He gestured to Taggart and the man took hold of The Doctor's mask and pulled it off his head, revealing his sweating, surly features.

'Well, well,' said McVeigh. 'William McSweeny!'

'You *know* him?' gasped Tom.

Taggart smiled. 'Oh, aye, we're old friends, aren't we, Willie? He's crossed our paths a few times before, usually for petty thieving and brawling. But this is a new departure for you, isn't it? Impersonating a doctor?' Taggart tutted loudly. 'I wouldn't be surprised if this latest venture takes your skinny neck in reach of a hangman's noose.'

'There's been a mistake,' argued McSweeny, struggling

to free himself 'I never said I was somebody I wasn't. I . . . I was only trying to help.'

'Help yourself more like,' said Taggart.

'You have to listen to me! I was a villain once, but these days I'm an honest man.'

'You wouldn't know honesty if it bit you on the backside,' said Taggart. He glanced at Lord Kelvin. 'Begging your pardon, Sir,' he added.

'Please don't trouble yourself,' said Lord Kelvin.

'Is your filthy old scarecrow of a mother still around?' asked Mcveigh 'And is she still drinking her own weight in neat gin every day?'

'You watch your mouth about my mother,' McSweeny warned him. He turned to look at Tom and his eyes blazed with hatred. 'You little snitch,' he hissed. 'You'd better sleep with one eye open from now on, boy, because I'll get you for this, you can depend on it. I will find you and I will destroy you. That is a promise.'

At that, the two constables turned him roughly around and propelled him towards the door which Millie was now holding open for them.

'All you'll be getting is bread and water,' observed McVeigh. 'Until they call you out for trial. And the day they hang you, Willie boy, I'll be there, dancing a jig as you drop.'

Then they were out of the door and bundling McSweeny's cloaked figure into their coach. They pushed him into a seat and positioned themselves on either side of him. As the coach moved away, he leaned forward and directed a cold glare through the open window to where

Tom was standing in the doorway. Tom could feel the venom in those eyes burning into him.

Lord Kelvin's hand came down on his shoulder, startling him.

'Well,' he said, 'after all that excitement, I think I could use another cup of tea. After that, we'll think about getting you home to Mistress Grierson's orphanage. She'll no doubt be worried about you.'

TWENTY-ONE

Tom lowered Lord Kelvin's letter, which he'd just finished reading aloud. He could see that there were tears in Missie Grierson's eyes and it seemed to take her considerable effort to find the right words.

'But . . . this is . . . incredible!' she said, at last 'I don't understand. What made him change his mind?'

'Meeting us,' said Cameron, beaming. 'He said if we were examples of the young men that were coming out of this place then he'd made a mistake turning us down. Isn't that so, Tom?'

Tom grinned, nodded. They were all in the kitchen of the orphanage. Morag was there and even Alison, dressed in her nightgown and with a blanket draped around her shoulders, had refused to stay in bed once she'd heard that Tom was back. Though still weak, she was well on her way to a full recovery, getting stronger every day. Missie Grierson had told Tom that they'd now had official permission to take the white sheet out of the window and that everything was getting back to normal. Or at least, it had been, until Tom and Cameron arrived with their incredible news.

'Did Lord Kelvin really say that?' gasped Missie Grierson, as though she couldn't believe her own ears. 'That he's going to try to find a place for us out in the country?'

Tom nodded. 'He says he's already got somewhere in mind,' he reminded her. 'You're to receive a proper wage as governess of the orphanage . . . and he's talking about you having more children . . . maybe twenty or thirty of them!'

The children were very excited at this news. 'I hope some of them are girls,' said Morag, nudging Alison. 'We'd like that, wouldn't we, Allie?'

'Well, that's all to be decided,' said Missie Grierson. 'We'll just have to wait and see. What was it he said in the letter, Tom?'

Tom glanced at it again. 'That he'll keep you informed of future developments.'

Missie Grierson beamed. 'You know what this means, children?' she cried. 'We'll no' have to take in any more laundry!'

There were murmurs of delight from everyone at this news.

'What do you suppose we'll do with our time?' asked Alison.

'We'll think of something,' Cameron assured her.

Missie Grierson looked at Tom. 'I don't know how you've managed to do this,' she said, 'but I thank you. I thank you from the bottom of my heart.'

'It wasn't just me,' Tom insisted. 'Cameron was there too. In fact, if he hadn't got me out of that cage, none of this would have happened.'

Cameron beamed and Morag came over to him and gave him a hug.

'You're no' so bad, after all,' she said. 'And I forgive you for punching Tom the way you did.'

'Ach, I still say he asked for it,' muttered Cameron, but he was grinning delightedly, basking in Morag's unexpected show of affection.

Missie Grierson sighed. 'Well,' she said, 'much as I hate to bring us all back down to earth, there's still the everyday duties to consider, at least for the time being. I need somebody to go to the market to collect the vegetables. Morag? We can hardly ask Tom or Cameron to go, after everything they've been through.'

'I'll go,' said Morag, walking across the kitchen and collecting the straw basket.

'I'll come with you,' offered Tom. He felt excited and restless and he wanted to be out in the hustle and bustle of the Close.

'Well, if you're sure,' said Missie Grierson. She turned to look at Alison. 'Let's get you back to bed,' she suggested. 'We don't want you overdoing things, not when you're on the mend.' Alison nodded and with an effort, got back on her feet. Missie Grierson guided her towards the stairs.

'I might just grab forty winks,' announced Cameron.

Missie Grierson eyed him. 'Don't push your luck,' she advised him.

Tom grinned and accompanied Morag out of the door and into the hall. They stepped outside into a brilliant summer's day and began to stroll along the cobbled street towards the market. As ever, the Close was packed with people, all pushing and shoving their way through the melee, but after everything that happened, it seemed boisterous and joyful.

'I thought you'd gone forever,' said Morag, falling into step with him. 'I couldn't believe it when you and Cameron turned up at the door, the way you did.' She smiled. 'Do you think he believes you now? About being from the future?'

Tom laughed. 'I doubt it,' he said. 'Cameron believes what Cameron wants to believe. He'll never change.'

They passed by the butcher's shop. On the road outside, another pig was hanging by its heels, a big pink creature, kicking and struggling against the ties that held it. As Tom and Morag went by, a man stooped and drew a sharp knife across the creature's throat. Blood spilled into the gutter. The man looked up at Tom and gave him a sly wink.

Tom felt a chill run through him. He felt suddenly nervous, unsettled. Something didn't feel right. He glanced quickly around at the swirling sea of faces surrounding him.

'What's the matter?' Morag asked him.

'Nothing,' he said, but he had the strong sense that something was wrong.

He carried on walking, trying to tell himself he was just being foolish, but he couldn't shake off the feeling of impending danger that was settling around him like a cold, clammy cloak.

'Are you sure, Tom? You've gone pale.'

'It's just . . . a feeling I've got.' He looked around again, and this time he caught a glimpse of somebody back in the crowd, somebody elbowing and jostling a way through the press of bodies. He had a brief impression of a dark, scowling face and a long leather cloak. The blood in his veins seemed to turn suddenly to ice. He put a hand on

Morag's shoulder and quickened his pace. She must have sensed the anxiety coming off him and she looked up at him in alarm.

'Tom, what is it?'

'Just keep walking,' he advised her. He glanced back over his shoulder, looking for another glimpse of that face, telling himself he must have been mistaken, because McSweeny had been arrested, there was no possibility of him wandering around the Close on this hot summer's day. And yet . . . and yet . . .

There he was again, closer now, pushing and shoving his way through the crowd, intent on catching up with Tom. Tom glanced at Morag, realising that she was in danger as long as she stayed with him.

'Morag, listen to me,' he said. 'I'm going to go a different way to you. I want you to carry on to the market.'

She stared at him. 'Why, Tom? Tell me what's wrong.'

'It's nothing, Morag, just . . . go, please, just do this for me.' He tried to branch left, away from her, but she came after him, clutching at his sleeve.

'Tom, what's wrong? Is it that bad man?' She was scanning the crowd herself now and he was terrified that something might happen to her.

'Morag, listen to me.' He crouched down and pulled her close. 'I have to go now, please try and understand. You can't be with me, now, you just can't. Now get going to that market, please!'

She stood there, staring at him, trying to fathom what the problem was, and then they both looked up at the sound of iron-capped boots, ringing on the cobbles.

McSweeny stood before them, a cold smile on his face. 'Tom,' he purred. 'Fancy meeting you here. I was just on my way to that orphanage of yours but now you've saved me the trouble.'

Tom got slowly back to his feet. He looked helplessly around at the crowds of people milling all around them. 'What are you doing here?' he murmured. 'I thought the constables . . .'

McSweeny laughed. 'You think constables are above temptation?' he smirked. 'I had fifty shillings in my purse. In this place, that's enough to bribe your way out of hell. They've given me twenty-four hours to get out of Edinburgh. But I thought to myself, I couldn't go without saying goodbye.'

'You . . . you can't do anything here,' said Tom. 'There are witnesses.'

McSweeny looked quickly around. 'You think they'll see anything?' He shook his head. 'Life is cheap on Mary King's Close,' he said. 'And most people prefer not to get involved.' He reached into his cloak and pulled out a long-bladed knife. 'I nearly took the constable's advice. I was all ready to get out of Edinburgh but then I thought to myself, what about young Tom? What about the little sneak who shopped me to the constables? Why not just come here first and kill you? It won't take long and it will make me feel so much better.'

Tom felt as though he was frozen to the spot. He glanced at Morag. 'Get away from here,' he whispered.

But she stood her ground, staring at McSweeny in disgust. 'You're a horrible man,' she said. 'I don't like you.'

McSweeny looked down at her, amused. 'Friend of yours?' he asked.

'She's nothing to do with this,' said Tom. 'Just let her go.'

'And why should I do that?' asked McSweeny, taking another step forward. 'Because that's what you want? At the moment, the thought of inflicting more pain on you seems very enticing.'

Tom reached out a hand to try and ease Morag behind him but she had ideas of her own. She broke away from his grasp and ran straight at McSweeny, swinging the straw basket like a weapon.

'Run, Tom!' she cried.

'Morag, no!' yelled Tom, horrified, but it was already too late. She flung herself at McSweeny and his right hand rose to meet her, the knife blade flashing dangerously, while his left arm encircled her waist and pulled her up close, as though for a hug. Morag's body flinched and stiffened and a gasp escaped from her lips. She went limp, like a puppet with severed strings, and slipped from McSweeny's grasp, collapsing onto the cobbles, her eyes wide and staring, a pool of dark red spreading across her apron.

'Tom,' she gasped, with what he somehow knew was the last breath she would ever take. 'Run!'

For Tom, the world seemed to stop turning. For an instant, everything was frozen in time: the Close, its inhabitants, McSweeny's cloaked figure and Morag's sprawled body. In that instant it occurred to him why he had first seen a ghost wandering in the corridors of Mary King's Close. It wasn't Annie whose presence haunted that room. It was Morag. She'd even been carrying the same straw basket she used to shop for vegetables.

Then everything slipped back into gear and McSweeny was stepping over the girl's body and coming for Tom. The knife in his hand was red with her blood.

'They arrested my mother,' he said as he approached. 'Did you know that, Tom? They took my poor seventy-one-year-old mother and threw her in a stinking prison, because she didn't have any money to bribe them with.'

He was close now, dangerously close. Suddenly, a switch in Tom's head seemed to snap on and he turned and ran into the heaving, pressing mass of the Close, pushing his way frantically through the sea of humanity, intent now only on escape. Behind him, he heard a voice yelling, 'Stop, thief!' and then people in the surrounding crowd were reaching out to grab at him, to hold him there until McSweeny could catch up. Somehow, he tore himself free and, spotting a ramshackle wooden door to his left, he veered towards it and shoved at it with both hands. It flew open and as he ran into the hallway beyond, his feet thudding on the bare floorboards, it struck him, in the midst of his panic, that he knew this place, this long, straight corridor, its plaster walls hung with dusty oil paintings he'd seen somewhere before . . . but not in this world.

Then it occurred to him. *Timeslyp*, the game he'd played so often on his phone. This was Level Six, the level he couldn't ever seem to get past and he knew that masked assassins were waiting for him in every shadow along this long, straight run. But he couldn't think about that now because he heard a thud behind him and, glancing back, he saw McSweeny had just come through the door in pursuit, his knife raised. There was no option but to run, to go down that hallway and try and make it to the next exit, impossibly distant at the far end of the corridor. Tom put his head down and launched himself forward.

Almost instantly, the first attacker came bursting through a painting to his right, a cloaked figure wearing a blank, smiling mask, a deadly, curved sickle clutched in one gloved hand. The man swung the sickle and Tom ducked instinctively, felt the razor-sharp blade skim the air inches above his head. He bobbed up again and struck the attacker full in his masked face, knocking him to the ground. He ran on, trying to remember where the next attack would come from and, even as he thought it, the assassin started to ooze up from below the floorboards: a flapping spectre wrapped in a black cloak, his upraised arms seeking to grab Tom's legs, his hands vaporous but quickly solidifying into flesh. Tom launched himself into the air, just evading the man's grasp and came down on the far side of him, his feet thudding as they struck wood. Behind him, he was aware of McSweeny's footsteps coming in pursuit.

He tried not to panic, telling himself that there were still three more attackers to evade before he reached the next door, and you never really knew the direction from which they would come. A man leapt from out of a painting to his left and he veered to one side and fended him away with one hand, slamming him down onto his face. In the same instant, a second man dived headlong from a painting on the right and Tom reacted instinctively, performing an agile forward roll beneath the flying figure, passing underneath him. Tom sprang to his feet and steeled himself for the final attack, knowing that this was the one he always misjudged. A sudden conviction seized him and he stopped dead in his tracks. The third attacker came hurtling down from above, sickle swinging. He struck the floor hard, with a gasp of exhaled air and Tom jumped onto his back and launched himself forward again, covering the last few yards to the door.

A sense of exaltation flashed through him. He'd done it. He'd reached the next level! His hands hit the door and it flew open.

He was in a room, a small empty room. Ahead of him was an open window, admitting the warm summer air. He could hear the sound of voices in the street outside. Tom ran to the window and looked out. To his right was the open street, crowded with people. His first instinct was to head that way, to lose himself in the crowd, but then a man in a tricorn hat saw him and shouted 'There! There's the thief!' and scores of angry faces turned to gaze at him.

Tom looked desperately to the left, saw a rickety wooden staircase leading up the side of the building and realised it was now his only avenue of escape. He heard McSweeny coming through the door behind him and knew he had no other choice. He climbed quickly out of the window, dropped to the ground and started up the stairs, three steps at a time. He was dimly aware of McSweeny struggling through the open window behind him.

'What's your hurry, Tom?' McSweeny cried as he clambered out and laboured up the stairs in pursuit. 'Come and see the nice surprise I've got for you!'

Tom kept going. A couple of women with painted faces were coming down the stairs arm-in-arm. He barged his way between them and gained the first landing. He went on up to the next level, his heart thudding like a mallet in his chest. He climbed the next flight, and the next, gazing up at the strip of bright blue sky far above him, wondering what he was supposed to do when he reached the very top. He glanced back and saw that McSweeny was still in hot pursuit, the knife held out in front of him, his leather cloak flapping behind him like the wings of a giant bat. Tom lunged around another flight and bumped into a portly man who was smoking a pipe on the staircase, sending him sprawling. Tom managed to scramble his way clear and went on, up to the fourth or fifth floor, he couldn't tell which. There were loud curses behind him as McSweeny also slammed into the fallen man.

'Get out of my way, you idiot!' he yelled and the thudding of those heavy boots continued. 'Tom!' he bellowed. 'What's the point of this? You know I'll get you in the end, why don't you accept your fate like a brave boy? That wee girl had more guts than you!'

Brave! thought Tom. That was a rich one. He thought of Morag lying dead on the cobbles and he wanted more than anything to turn and fight, but he knew he wouldn't stand a chance against a powerful man armed with a knife. He glanced desperately over the stair rail and saw a sea of heads swarming below him, a few faces upturned to look at what was going on far above them. He wondered about jumping. If he did that, would there be enough people down there to break his fall?

Tom pounded up to the next level, realising as he did so that this was just about as far as he could go. He reached the top of the stairs and stood there, gasping for breath. He looked to his left and saw a stretch of flat roof ahead of him, a patchwork quilt of rain-rotted timber and cracked tiles and crumbling chimney stacks.

McSweeny was coming up the last flight, a smile of triumph on his thin lips, while his eyes glittered with dark malevolence. 'Oh, dear, Tom,' he panted. 'That seems to be ... as far as you can go. If I were you, I'd ... make my peace with the world; you're not much longer for it.'

Tom took a deep breath and stepped carefully off the top of the stairs onto the nearest stretch of roof. Ancient timbers creaked as they sagged beneath his weight but he kept going, trying to spot the stronger sections. If he could reach the far side, there might be another staircase leading down. McSweeny paused at the top of the stairs and leaned on the rail, getting his breath back.

'Don't you understand, Tom? This is how it's all meant to end. You and me. It's destiny. The first time I laid eyes on you, I knew. I somehow just *knew* it would end like this. There are people you meet and you somehow know that one day you'll end up killing them.'

He took a cautious step out onto the roof, judging the creaking of the wood beneath him. He seemed satisfied. He began to walk forward and Tom cautiously backed away.

'Look,' said Tom. 'This is crazy. How is killing me going to help anything?'

'Well, it'll make me feel happier, for one thing. It's

nothing personal, Tom. It's just the way of the world. You've dealt me a bad hand of cards and that can't be ignored . . .'

'I dealt *you* the cards?' Tom snorted in disbelief. 'I didn't do anything wrong! You . . . you came to the orphanage, you took me, you . . . you stole the pills from me, and then you got caught for doing something bad. How is any of that supposed to be my fault?'

McSweeny edged closer, the blade held out in front of him. 'You let me down,' he said. 'I chose you as my accomplice and you should have been honoured. But no, you threw it in my face . . . and then you went sneaking around behind my back, telling your wee stories, turning everyone against me . . .'

Tom edged backwards a little more and realised that behind him there was a wide expanse of dirty glass, many of the panes cracked and discoloured. A skylight. He didn't dare try to put his weight on that. He began to edge to his left instead.

'What's the matter, Tom?' murmured McSweeny. 'Gone as far as you can go? Realise you've reached the end of the road?' His knife arm came back a little, as though seeking a target. 'Well, you tried, boy, but you can't evade your destiny forever. There comes a time when you have to account for what you've done . . . and that time is at hand.'

And then he lunged, thrusting his right arm forward with all the power he could muster. Tom leaned back, balanced precariously on the edge of the skylight as the blade swung a deadly arc, just inches from his throat. He felt himself falling and instinctively grabbed hold of McSweeny's outstretched arm, pulling him off-balance too. For a moment, they swayed like dancers on the edge of disaster. Tom threw up his left arm and wrapped it around McSweeny's neck, telling himself that, if he was going to fall, he wasn't going to do it alone. McSweeny swore under his breath as the weight of Tom's body twisted him around, and then they were turning as they fell towards the glass.

McSweeny hit it first and Tom came down on top of him. For a moment, the surface held and they lay there unsure of what to do – then there was a shattering sound and the glass broke up beneath them and they were plunging into darkness; dust and debris raining around them.

They seemed to fall for a very long time before McSweeny slammed against a hard unyielding surface. Tom felt the man's body spasm beneath him and a warm wetness pulsed over his hand. Tom realised that in the struggle, the knife had somehow gone into McSweeny's chest. He was staring up at Tom, an expression of surprise, on his ghastly white face.

'You!' he hissed. 'You've . . . killed me . . .'

Tom tried to struggle off McSweeny but the body beneath him had no substance, it was collapsing beneath him like a deflated balloon, it was dissolving, fading, until it was completely gone and there was nothing between him and the debris-covered floor.

He got himself onto his knees and tried to stand, but he felt sick and dizzy and the empty room began to swoop and spin around him like a great, dusty carousel, moving faster and faster. He tried to take a step but his foot seemed to sink into the dirt floor beneath him and a great white light blossomed like fire at the back of his skull and spread throughout him, until it obliterated everything.

Then the world turned black.

TWENTY-TWO

Tom opened his eyes and, for a moment, was dazzled by a glare of lights. He blinked violently and became aware of a series of blurred shapes around him that gradually swam into focus. He was lying in bed, his head propped up by thick, clean-smelling pillows. A dark blur to his left slowly became something solid and he saw that a man was sitting beside the bed, reading a newspaper.

'Dad?'

Tom's voice emerged as a kind of strangled croak and Dad dropped the paper as though he'd been electrocuted.

'Tom!' He leaned closer to the bed. 'You're awake! Thank God. We've all been so worried about you.'

Tom blinked again, trying to put it together. He moved his head from one side to the other, taking in the scene. He was in a small hospital room. Beside him, machinery beeped and chugged rhythmically. Various wires led from him to the machines but he couldn't work out exactly how he was attached to them.

'What . . . what's happened?' he croaked.

'Just a moment.' Dad got up from the chair and pressed a button on a length of wire. Then he picked up a plastic tumbler of water from the bedside locker. He lifted it to Tom's mouth and let him take a couple of small sips from it. 'Not too much,' he advised. 'Got to take it slowly.' He set the tumbler back down on the locker. A door opened and a young nurse looked into the room. 'He's awake,' Dad told her.

'I'll get Doctor Wilson,' she said and closed the door again.

Dad slipped back into his seat and smiled at Tom. 'How much do you remember?' he asked.

Tom shook his head and then wished he hadn't, because it made him feel dizzy. 'I was . . . I think . . . I went to Mary King's Close,' he said. 'A school trip. Yes. We went this morning.'

Dad shook his head. 'No, Tom. That happened three days ago,' he said. 'You've been unconscious since then.'

'Three . . . three days?' Now Tom became aware of a dull ache at the top of his head. He lifted a hand to find that it was covered by a thick layer of bandages.

'Better not touch that, son,' said Dad. 'Let's wait until the doctor gets here.'

'The Doctor?' Tom looked at Dad in alarm. 'I don't want to see The Doctor!' He tried to sit up but Dad placed a hand gently against his chest and eased him back against his pillows.

'Calm down,' he said. 'Of course you have to see him. He's got to check that everything's OK.' He looked at Tom. 'So that's all you remember?' he asked. 'Going on the school trip?'

'I . . . well, I remember going into this room and then, the floor gave way . . .'

Dad was shaking his head. 'That's not what they told me!' he protested. 'They said you tried to go into a room with a low lintel and you bashed your head on it. It wasn't even part of the tour; nobody can work out what you were doing there.'

'I was following Morag,' said Tom.

'Morag? Is that one of the girls from your class?'

'No . . . she was sort of all flickery . . .'

Dad looked baffled. 'Your teacher said you were on your own. You'd left the others and gone wandering off.' He waved a hand, as though dismissing the details. 'That doesn't matter,' he said. 'You're awake again; that's the most important thing. Everybody's been so worried about you.'

Tom sighed and then gestured for more water. Dad got the tumbler and lifted it to his mouth again. Tom's mouth felt drier than sand. It seemed to absorb the mouthfuls of water like blotting paper. He swallowed gratefully then lay there for a moment, trying to gather his thoughts.

'So . . . is this real?' he asked. 'Or just another alternate reality?'

Dad frowned. 'You're not making a lot of sense, son,' he said.

'Because there's been other realities,' said Tom, trying to explain. 'I kept coming back but everything was different. You were driving a BMW.'

'Was I?' Dad looked impressed. 'Chance would be a fine thing.'

Tom looked at Dad for a moment. 'So . . . what are you doing here?' he asked.

'What do you think? Obviously I came as soon as I heard what had happened to you.'

'I thought you couldn't take time off work?'

'Sod that, some things are more important. I've squared it with my boss, anyway; he was very understanding. Told me to take as long as I needed. I got straight in the car and drove for five hours solid.'

'But, what . . .?'

'In a way, it took this to make me wake up, Tom. To make me realise that I couldn't just let things go on the way they were. This happening, it's knocked some sense back into me and your Mum. We've had to straighten things out between us.'

'You're . . . getting back together?'

Dad shook his head. 'It's too late for that, Tom. What happened between us, it's . . . well, it's sad of course, but life goes on and your Mum shouldn't have involved you the way she did. I told her that she couldn't just take you and run off. How irresponsible was that? And I told her there are two parents in this situation, not just her. I said I wasn't going to take it lying down and that you're old enough now to know your own mind. She argued with me, of course she did, but in the end, she had to agree that I was right.'

'So . . . where *is* Mum?'

'We've been taking it in turns to sit with you. This just happens to be my shift. She'll be along in an hour or so.'

Tom nodded. His head was becoming clearer by the second. He was pretty sure now this wasn't an alternate reality. He was really beginning to think it was actually happening. 'So . . . what now?' he asked.

'That's up to you, Tom. You have the choice. Come back to Manchester with me or stay here with your Mum and . . .

her new bloke. Wherever you choose to stay, we'll arrange it so that you can have regular contact with both of us, whenever you want. But we'll do it through the courts so it's all properly sorted. In the end, it has to be your choice, son. You're not a baby any more.'

'I'm coming with you,' said Tom, without hesitation.

'Are you sure? You're not just saying that because I'm sitting here in front of you?'

Tom shook his head. 'I miss my friends. I miss my room. And I hate it in Hamish's place. It feels . . . like I'm in the way, the whole time.' He scowled. 'There are Hibs posters on my bedroom wall!'

Dad pulled a face. 'Nasty,' he said.

'So, if it's OK with you, I want to go back to Manchester.'

Dad nodded, smiled. 'I'm glad,' he said. 'Really glad. And Tom, I'll try to sort everything out for you, but if I get things wrong, you just have to tell me, OK? And then I'll try a bit harder.' He put a hand on Tom's shoulder. 'When Mum gets here and you're feeling stronger, we'll have a good talk about this. You can tell Mum what you've decided.'

Tom scowled. 'Do I have to?' he muttered.

'Yes, I think it's for the best.' Dad looked at Tom. 'Whatever you think about her, Tom, she didn't stop loving you. She's still your mum.'

Tom nodded. 'I want to come back here too,' he said. 'For holidays and stuff. To see Mum. And to find out more about Edinburgh. It's a really cool place.'

Dad looked surprised. 'You really think so?'

Tom smiled. 'Oh yes,' he said. 'It has . . . hidden depths.'

Just then, the door opened and a figure stepped into the room. Tom steeled himself, anticipating the worst, but Doctor Wilson was just a young man in a white coat, with a face that Tom had never seen before.

'So, the sleeper finally awakes,' he said, in a soft Edinburgh accent. He approached the bed. 'You gave everyone a proper scare,' he said. 'How are you feeling?'

'Confused,' said Tom.

'I'll bet you are. That was quite a bash on the noggin you gave yourself. Had us all very worried for a while.' He took a small torch from his pocket and switched it on, started moving it left and right in front of Tom's face. 'Follow the light with your eyes,' he said and, after a few moments, he seemed satisfied with Tom's efforts.

'Excellent,' he said. 'I was pretty sure you'd wake up before long but three days was pushing it. I was starting to think we might have more of a problem on our hands. What do you remember about the accident?'

'I already asked him that,' said Dad. 'He said something about . . . falling through the floor?'

Doctor Wilson shook his head. 'No, I'm pretty sure he just bumped his head.' He smiled. 'Any dreams?' he asked.

'Dreams?' Tom looked at him. 'Yes! The weirdest dreams. But not like dreams, more like they were really happening. I went back to the seventeenth century. But I kept coming back to now, and things were different.' He looked at Dad. 'You were an architect,' he said. 'And Mum worked for the BBC!'

Dad and the doctor exchanged looks and laughed.

'But I kept being pulled back to Mary King's Close . . .

not the way it is now. In the seventeenth century. People had the plague and I had to work with The Doctor . . .' He looked at Doctor Wilson. 'Not you,' he added. 'A plague doctor. He wore this weird outfit . . . made him look like a big bird.'

Now Dad was looking anxiously at Doctor Wilson, but he just smiled and shook his head. 'It's quite common in cases of severe concussion,' he said. 'It's almost as though the brain creates these things in order to keep itself active, to stop itself from shutting down.' He moved to the machines and studied the screens for a few moments. 'Everything here looks just as it should,' he said. 'I think Tom's been very lucky. But obviously, we'll keep him in for another day or so, for observation, just until we're absolutely sure there's no damage.'

Dad let out a sigh of relief. 'Thanks, Doc,' he said.

'No worries. Now, I suggest you let him sleep a bit more. He's still groggy and it really is the best thing for him right now. From the look of you, I'd say you could use a little sleep yourself.'

Dad nodded. 'I'll just say goodbye, if that's OK. And I'll wait outside until his mother gets here.'

'Of course.' Doctor Wilson smiled at Tom and left the room, closing the door behind him.

'Sounds like you had quite an adventure,' said Dad.

Tom nodded. 'Yeah,' he said. 'Yeah, I did. Dad, I wouldn't mind calling at Mary King's Close again before we head back to Manchester.'

Dad raised his eyebrows. 'Really? Want to see if you can give yourself a bigger bump on the head?'

Tom shook his head. 'I want to buy a doll and leave it for . . . for the ghost.'

Dad grimaced. 'The place sounds a bit creepy,' he said.

'It's not,' Tom assured him. 'It's more . . . atmospheric.'

'Well,' said Dad, looking around. 'Whatever you want. I'd say you've earned a couple of treats. I'd better let you get some rest now. If you need anything, me or your Mum will be out in the waiting room. And if you feel sick or anything, just press the button.'

He got to his feet and then seemed to remember something else. He reached into his pocket and pulled out Tom's mobile.

'Oh, yes, this was in your blazer pocket when they brought you in. I charged it up for you. Thought you might be glad of it when you're feeling a bit better. You can play that game you like so much.'

'*Timeslyp*,' said Tom. 'Thanks, Dad.'

Dad put the mobile on Tom's locker and went out of the room. Tom lay there, listening to the rhythmic sounds from the machine beside him, a strangely comforting lullaby. He felt tiredness plucking at him with insistent fingers and he was almost ready to surrender, to go down into it. He had never felt more exhausted in his entire life. But a sudden thought occurred to him. With an effort, he reached out a hand and picked up the mobile, then pulled it to him. He pressed the power button. He stared at the screen for a moment, not quite knowing what he expected to find. He took a breath and pressed the icon that opened up the photo app. The screen filled instantly with the last picture he had taken.

He lay there looking at it. It was Morag. She was sitting in a chair in Missie Grierson's dingy kitchen and there was a questioning look on her face. Her mouth was open as if she were saying something. Tom seemed to remember that she'd been asking him what he was doing. He smiled. He didn't know what to think about this. He considered calling for Dad; he could show him the picture and tell him how it had come to be on the phone, so he could try to explain everything in detail. But then he imagined Dad's worried expression, how he might think that maybe Tom wasn't so well after all, that the blow to the head had caused permanent damage. He didn't want to worry anyone . . . and besides, right now it was all too much effort. He was so tired. So very tired.

His eyelids came down like a pair of shutters. The phone slipped out of his hand and fell onto the bed covers beside him.

He slept. And this time there were no nightmares waiting for him.

Children's Books

Sebastian Darke: Prince of Fools
Sebastian Darke: Prince of Pirates
Sebastian Darke: Prince of Explorers
Sebastian Darke: Prince of Spies
A Buffalope's Tale

Alec Devlin: The Eye of the Serpent
Alec Devln: Empire of the Skull
Alec Devlin: Maze of Death

Movie Maniacs: Night On Terror Island
Movie Maniacs: Spy Another Day
Movie Maniacs: Space Blasters (coming May 2013)

Cursery Rhymes (with Bob Seal)

Seventeen Coffins
One for Sorrow
The Watchers
The Calling

Adult Thrillers

The Sins Of Rachel Ellis
Tiger, Tiger
The Tarantula Stone
Speak No Evil
Black Wolf
Strip Jack Naked
Slayground
Skin Flicks
Burn Down Easy
Bad To The Bone
1999

The last gripping instalment in
the Sebastian Darke series.